HOUSTON
ATTACK

HOUSTON ATTACK

RANDY WAYNE
WHITE
WRITING AS CARL RAMM

OPEN ROAD
INTEGRATED MEDIA
NEW YORK

Cover design by Andy Ross

ISBN: 978-1-5040-3518-7

This edition published in 2016 by Open Road Integrated Media, Inc.
180 Maiden Lane
New York, NY 10038
www.openroadmedia.com

HOUSTON ATTACK

ONE

The bar was on the Mexican side of the Rio Grande. It was built of concrete block on a concrete slab in a border town where the desert pressed hard against the slum housing and tequila joints.

The bar had once been painted a fluorescent green. But the Mexican sun had leached the color from it, and now, beneath its red neon sigh, the building looked gray in the summer darkness.

Las Almas Desconocidas.

A fitting name for such a bar, thought James Hawker.

The Bar of the Unknown Souls.

Hawker pulled the hat down low over his eyes and went inside.

The bar was crowded. No one seemed to notice the tall one-armed stranger. He stumbled and tottered his way to the bar, obviously drunk.

Anywhere else the serape and the sweat-ruined cattleman's hat he wore would have looked ludicrous.

But not here.

The place was crammed with Mexican ranch hands and a few Texas cowboys who had crossed the border to blow their month's pay on whores and tequila.

The bartender was a hugely fat Latin with black hair that came to his shoulders. He wore a soiled apron, and there was a tattoo on the back of his hand.

He looked at the stranger expectantly.

"Mescal," the stranger said, as if through numb lips. "*Una botella.*"

The bartender slid the bottle in front of him. "Save your bad Spanish." He said with a sneer. "The mescal is two hundred pesos. The entertainment is another hundred."

At the front of the bar was a low stage. The two speakers above the stage blasted out a Mexican version of "The Stripper." There was a chair in the middle of the stage, and a lanky Anglo woman was bent naked over it.

She wore a blond wig, and her breasts were thin and tubular, scarred by stretch marks.

A very muscular black man slathered oil over her buttocks, occasionally burying his fist inside her. Beside the black man was tied a gigantic male Great Dane.

The woman's expression was worn and vacant, her eyes glazed by drugs.

As the black man untied the dog, the stranger turned away.

He emptied the glass of mescal and said to the bartender, "I was told that a man who wanted to get back into the United States should come here."

The bartender eyed him carefully and moved closer.

"You're drunk," he said.

The stranger swallowed the second glass of mescal. "I have money. I'm not asking for any favors. I can pay."

"You're a gringo. Why should a gringo need help getting into the United States?"

The stranger carefully reached across with his left hand and pulled out the empty right shirt-sleeve from beneath the serape. "I have made enemies of the police there. They have taken this much of me. I wish to give them no more."

The bartender nodded thoughtfully, then disappeared through a door behind the bar into the next room.

The stranger waited. He pretended to gulp another glass of mescal. He wobbled on his stool as if about to pass out.

The bartender returned in a few minutes. The stranger knew that other men had studied him carefully through the two-way mirror behind the rows of liquor bottles.

The bartender leaned close to him. "This thing you ask, it can be done. But it is only at great risk to certain friends of mine. They must be paid for their risks."

The stranger belched and nodded. "I was told ten thousand pesos."

"You were told wrong," the bartender snapped. "It is twenty thousand, plus a thousand pesos for me." He smiled for the very first time, an ugly cigarette-stained smile. "I, too, run risks—as the *intermediaro*."

The stranger shook his head. He knew that if he agreed immediately to the price, they might suspect him of being an undercover agent. "Far too much," he said. "I do not have that kind of money." He got down off the barstool carefully. "I am sorry. I was given the wrong information. I have come to the wrong place." He picked up the bottle of mescal as if to take it with him.

"Wait," the bartender said quickly. When the stranger turned to listen, he added, "These things can be negotiated. You leave too easily."

The stranger leaned his weight against the bar. "I was told ten thousand pesos."

"Too little, too little, amigo. Have another drink and we will discuss—"

"I will give you fifteen hundred pesos for your help, and another ten thousand for your friends who take the great risks."

The ugly smile returned to the bartender's face. He leaned, whispering. "When do you wish to leave?"

"As soon as possible."

"Tonight?"

The stranger nodded. "Yes. Tonight."

"There is a truck with a long trailer behind the bar," the bartender whispered. "Go down the hall to the *cuarto de baño*—the bathroom. A man will meet you there. You will leave in the truck." The bartender held out his hand. "But first, you pay."

The stranger stabbed his hand into his pocket and brought out a roll of bills. "I will pay you your fifteen hundred now. The rest I will pay to the man with the truck."

The bartender sighed, disgusted. The stranger was drunk, but he was no fool.

Behind them the roomful of men suddenly broke into loud

hoots and whistles of approval at something they saw on the stage.

The bartender thought it odd that the stranger did not even turn to look.

The restroom of the Mexican bar stank of urine and sour beer.

The stranger waited outside, slumped in his serape, trying to look smaller than he was.

A door at the back of the building opened, and two men came toward him.

"You pay us," the bigger of the two said. "You give us the money, and we put you on the truck." He held out his hand impatiently.

The stranger eyed them warily. "When I'm on the truck— that's when I'll pay you."

The two Mexican men looked at each other and broke into wolfish chuckles. They found the defiance of this drunken American laughable. There was really no need for him to pay them the money, for they planned to take all his money, anyway.

"As you wish," said the largest Mexican. "You pay us when we put you on the truck."

The stranger considered the mescal bottle for a moment, holding it up to the bare light bulb that protruded from the ceiling. There was just a little left, and he emptied the bottle with one gulp before dropping it on the floor.

The glass shattered across the concrete.

The two Mexicans, still smiling, looked at each other and nodded knowingly.

The stranger took two wobbly steps toward the door before collapsing. He knew that pretending to pass out was less painful than being knocked out by the blackjack the smaller Mexican was doing a bad job of hiding.

He felt them go through his pockets and take the money.

He was thankful they didn't search beneath the serape. The roll of peso notes had been enough to convince them he carried no hidden stash. But money wasn't what he was afraid of their finding.

They dragged him by the feet through the doorway and across the back lot. There was the metallic sound of a deadbolt being opened, and then he was pulled roughly up onto the sheet-metal bedding of a semi-tractor-trailer truck. There was the sound of cardboard boxes being moved away, and then the stranger felt his left hand being handcuffed to the wall of the truck, as he'd known it would be.

The big Mexican made a joke about his having only one arm, and where they might latch the other handcuff.

Before they left, they gave rough orders in rapid Spanish. The stranger heard the meek replies of voices he had not heard before.

He was not the only one chained in the truck.

Finally the trailer's door slammed closed, and James Hawker opened his eyes.

Out of some unexpected courtesy they had left a small battery-operated lamp burning. The soft golden light made the trailer seem cavernlike. Hawker studied the men and women with him. There were about twenty—all handcuffed to the trailer wall. They sat uncomfortably on the floor, watching him.

Except for him, they were all Latins or Indios. Their ages varied, but none were old. They all looked to be younger than fifty and in good health.

It made sense.

The Texas land barons who were behind this organization didn't want any old slaves.

Like the livestock on their massive ranches, they wanted the people they kidnapped into slavery to be young and sleek and fit.

Hawker sat up and pushed his western hat back. He scanned the faces staring at him.

"Does anyone here speak English?" he asked calmly.

There was a long silence. It was obvious that none of them had expected to see an Anglo among them.

"It's okay," he said gently. "I'd like to help you, if I can."

A girl who sat across from him hesitated, then said in perfect English, "How could you possibly help? You are chained just as we are." She made a face of distaste. "And you smell like . . . like you've taken a bath in tequila."

Hawker smiled and threaded his right arm back through his shirt-sleeve and brought it from beneath his serape. "Mescal," he said as he reached down into his sock and fished out a ring of handcuff master keys. "It was mescal I took a bath in, not tequila." He looked at her and winked. "I guess it's to your credit that you can't tell the difference."

Her cheeks flushed as Hawker began to try the keys one by one on the single cuff that held him. She had one of those age-less Mayan faces. High cheek-bones. Nut-colored skin. Onyx-black hair that hung down over the surprisingly ripe bosom swell. Hawker guessed her to be about eighteen, though she could have been thirty just as easily. But Indio women tend to get chubby and domestic when they hit their mid-twenties, and there was nothing chubby about this one. She was long and lithe, and Hawker could see that she had been crying.

"What's your name?" he asked.

"Cristoba. Cristoba de Abella."

"Do you know where they're taking you, Cristoba?" Hawker asked after telling her his own name.

Her chin trembled slightly. She shook her head. "All I know is that I was waiting on a bus to take me back to the University of Mexico in Mexico City when those . . . those *bastards* shoved me in a car, and then they stuck me with something . . . a needle, I guess . . . and then I woke up here."

"How long ago was that?"

"I have no idea."

"What was it like—the stuff they stuck you with?"

The girl averted her eyes from his for the first time. "It knocked me out. That's all I know."

"No, it didn't," Hawker pressed. "The stuff they gave you felt good. You liked it."

Her face crinkled and she burst suddenly into tears. "You act like I *wanted* them to do it. *Yes*, it made me feel good, dammit! But I don't know what it was! I just want to go home. . . ."

The girl sagged away, swinging slightly on the handcuffs that held her. The other Mexicans and Indios in the trailer began to speak fast Spanish at Hawker, and their looks were threatening. Who was this nasty Anglo to upset this poor, pretty girl who already had enough trouble?

Hawker still worked furiously at his cuffs, trying key after key. If none of the hundred and twenty-seven keys worked, he would have to use the tiny hacksaw blade he had brought.

As he worked at the cuffs he spoke to the girl. "I'm not accusing you of anything, Cristoba," he said softly. "And there's no reason for you to feel guilty. They gave you heroin. In a way, I guess, you should feel flattered. They don't waste it on everyone. Only the very strong and the very valuable. They want to have a hook in you so the person who buys you can be sure you'll stick around."

The girl's quick intake of air was like a whispered scream. "*Sell* me?" Her hand went to her mouth. "Oh, my God, you don't really mean that?"

Finally Hawker found the right key. The lone handcuff snapped open, and he rubbed his wrist to get the blood flowing again. "I'm afraid I do," he said. "And I want you to tell the others what is planned for them. They're going to drive this truck back into the United States. The border guards have already been paid. By early tomorrow we'll be somewhere within a hundred miles of Houston. Just after sunrise a very small and elite group of Texas land barons are going to have an auction."

Hawker looked deep into her eyes. "Most of the men and women in this truck will be sold as field hands and house servants. Like me, they paid the bartender inside that rat-hole bar to find them a way to gain entry into the U.S. illegally. But a girl as young and beautiful as you will bring top price, and it won't be because those bastards think you're a good cook. That's why they gave you the heroin. And that's why they're going to keep giving it to you until you're hooked so completely that you'd never give a thought to running away from your only source of the stuff."

For a second Hawker thought the girl was going to break into tears again. But then her face became a stoic mask, and her brown eyes burned. She jerked at her cuffs. "Get me out of these," she hissed. "Let me loose. Free us all, and the moment they open that door—"

"I can't," Hawker cut in. "Those two Mexican guards are almost sure to check us one more time before they pull out."

"But you've freed yourself!"

"Keep your voice down, Cristoba," Hawker whispered calmly. "I'll fix my cuff so it looks like it's still locked, and they'll think I'm still passed out, so they won't even bother to check me. But I can't take that chance with the others. Don't you see? We have to make this trip tonight. I have to find out where they're taking you people and who's involved. Sure, I could probably fight our way out of here right now. But that's not going to help the people they've already kidnapped—and the people they'll kidnap in the future. When they've taken us to the very source of this slavery ring, Cristoba, I'll free you." Hawker leaned across the truck and patted her warm shoulder gently. "You'll be safe with me. I promise you that. But I have to do it my own way."

The girl leaned her weight briefly against his hand. Her head was bowed shyly, and she looked up at him. "There is something in your eyes that I trust."

"And you understand?"

"I understand."

"Then tell the others, Cristoba. Tell them what I have

planned, and tell them to obey my every gesture. If they do, we've got a chance to get out of this thing safely—"

Hawker was interrupted by the sound of the truck starting: a sputtering diesel roar. And then the bolt on the trailer door slammed open, and the two Mexicans shoved the boxes away.

Hawker settled back beneath his hat, as if still unconscious. He expected them to check a few of the cuffs and take a head count.

But that's not what happened.

He heard an unfamiliar voice yelling in Spanish, and just as it came to him that one of the "slaves" handcuffed with him in the truck was really a plant, he heard Cristoba de Abella scream, "James, look out! They know!"

Hawker jerked his left hand free from its chain while sliding his right hand beneath the serape. He rolled hard across the trailer deck as two ear-shattering explosions ricocheted slugs off the metal floor behind him.

He heard a familiar scream, and his peripheral vision registered that the beautiful Indian girl's arm now oozed blood as she writhed beneath her chains.

Hawker brought his customized Colt Commander .45 to bear on the face of the smaller of the two Mexican guards and squeezed the trigger.

The revolver the Mexican had been holding slammed against the ceiling as his thick face splattered gore. The scream that had materialized on his lips was never uttered as the impact of the heavy .45 slug jolted his head back, broke his neck, and knocked his corpse to the floor.

In the same instant the bigger of the two Mexicans charged Hawker and kicked the Colt savagely from his hand.

Hawker tackled him around the ankles and wrestled him to the deck. The Mexican brought his revolver up to fire, but Hawker twisted it away with his left hand while putting all his weight behind a right fist that crushed the man's throat closed.

The Mexican's eyes bulged, and his feet kicked wildly on the deck as his throat hissed, fighting for air.

"James, look out!" screamed Cristoba de Abella.

The warning was unnecessary. The man who had obviously been planted inside the trailer to keep an eye on the kidnap victims was a huge man with massive shoulders. Earlier Hawker had noticed him only in passing: a man who looked like a prime slave candidate for the fields.

Now he was kneeling to pick up the revolver that had been knocked from the smaller Mexican's hands.

Hawker jumped to his feet and charged him. In the same instant he felt the truck jolt as some unseen driver—probably aware that they now had trouble—shoved it into gear and began to pull away.

Hawker hit the big man with a waist-high tackle, knocking him into the wall nearest the double doors. There was the heavy, reassuring clatter of the revolver hitting the deck. Hawker drew back his right fist to swing, but before he got the punch off, the big man nailed him with a crushing blow to the chest that ignited popping blue lights in Hawker's head.

Hawker heard a second punch whistle past his ear and bang off the aluminum siding of the trailer.

A thin hiss of pain escaped the man's lips, and Hawker realized that he had probably broken his hamlike hand. Hawker slammed his elbow into the man's ribs, then hit him with a cracking overhand right that would have knocked out any ordinary man.

But not this man.

Hawker hit him with a rapid series of punches to the body, then slid under a powerful left hook. It was hard to keep his balance now, because the truck was gaining speed, pulling away.

Hawker locked his arms around the man's heavy waist and tried to trip him to the deck. The man launched an elbow at Hawker's head, and as the vigilante ducked away, the sudden shift in momentum sent them both crashing against the double doors of the trailer.

There was a tremendous impact, and Hawker was aware of the doors opening and then of being airborne, flying through the night.

With a searing jolt he hit the asphalt highway, and then he was rolling through gravel. James Hawker got shakily but quickly to his feet, ready to continue the fight with the Mexican.

But the huge shape in the middle of the road did not stir. The Mexican was knocked out cold by the fall or dead.

Hawker hoped that he was dead.

Experimentally Hawker moved both his arms and then his legs. Nothing seemed to be broken.

They had been carried about three hundred yards from the bar, and Hawker was aware of men running toward him. There was the muted flash and cough of gunfire and the nearby whiz of lead slugs scraping the highway.

They were shooting at him.

North on the desert highway, the semi-tractor-trailer's lights were bright, taunting eyes as the truck sped its slaves toward Texas.

Hawker's words to the girl haunted him: "You'll be safe with me. I promise you that."

Right.

Somehow he had to find her. Somehow he had to save her from the living hell that awaited her and the others.

As the men running toward him grew nearer Hawker threw back the serape and unstrapped the brutal-looking little Ingram submachine gun.

He couldn't allow himself to think about the girl now. Before he could save her, first he had to survive. . . .

TWO

As James Hawker waited on the tarmac, waited in the balmy Mexican night for his attackers to fall within range of the Ingram, he thought, It can't end here. I've worked too hard tracking these bastards down, worked too many lonely weeks to see them slip through my fingers. Plus, there's now the girl to consider . . . if she lives. . . .

It had been his most unusual assignment to date.

And one of his toughest.

He had spent a long winter in Chicago doing a dangerously good imitation of the stereotypical suburban male. He had allowed himself to be sucked into the cozy trap that cold weather so easily sets: It's ten below outside, so let's just skip the run and calisthenics today . . . and tomorrow . . . and next week. There's a hell of a blizzard blowing in, so why not curl up on the couch and watch a little television. With a beer, maybe . . . and a couple of sandwiches now that you're in the kitchen . . . and maybe a piece of pie, too, because you don't want to hurt the landlady's feelings.

It had gone on and on like that, through January and February, and then into the long, gray sopping month of March.

And he deserved it, didn't he?

He'd put his damn neck on the line too many times during the last assignment: that run-in with the Nazis of New York and their crazy plan to rebuild the Third Reich.

And he'd damn near lost one of his best friends to boot: Jacob Montgomery Hayes.

It had been Hayes's idea to put Hawker's unique cop skills to work in a nation that was quickly being destroyed by crooks and killers and con artists who no longer feared—or needed to fear—the American court system.

It had been Hayes's idea to seek out selected areas of the nation where innocent people were being bullied and then send in Hawker to help them fight back.

Hayes, one of the richest men in the world, would provide whatever financial backing was needed.

Hawker would provide the experience, the muscle, and the street sense.

And it had gone well. Almost too well. None of the missions had been easy, but they had all been successful . . . until they ran into the Nazis of New York.

It was the first mission in which Hayes had gotten personally involved. And it had almost cost him his life. Hawker and the inimitable butler, Hendricks, had spent long nights by Hayes's bedside, waiting while he hung by a thread between life and death.

But finally the tough old Texas billionaire started to come around. Started to respond to the nursing and the around-the-clock doctors' care. Started to draw on the innate stubbornness that had driven him from the poverty of his south Texas youth to the top of the business ladder and far, far beyond.

Hayes began to heal, and then he began to get crotchety, souring in bed. And when they finally let him get up, his old good humor began to return, and then he began reading his esoteric books on Zen and began tying his beloved trout flies, and finally Jacob was his old, sweet, imposing self.

And that's when winter set in and Hawker used the weather as an excuse to go on his extended vacation.

After a month of too much rest and too much food, he made a couple of halfhearted efforts to get back into shape. Each effort started with a muscle-wearying flurry, then ground to a slow halt.

After about the fourth failed attempt, Hawker began to get scared.

He knew all about the sweet trap of middle age: eat when you feel like it; drink all you want; and someday, when the time is right, get back into shape because there's always time. . . .

Someday. But Hawker had too many old friends who lived for "someday." They were overweight and out of shape, and because they took little pride in their own physical well-being, they took little pride in their lives. To wait for "someday" Hawker knew was to settle for that slow decline that led only to the coffin.

And James Hawker had no desire to die of old age.

So, on a bleak March morning, he put himself back on the old routine. No excuses. No whining. And damn the wind, snow, and rain.

He started slowly, feeling the fat bounce on his sides during the morning run, feeling the deteriorated muscles burning during the hour of calisthenics. Feeling the shame of the slowed reflexes during the brutal sparring sessions at the old Bridgeport gym.

But he stuck with it. And by April he was beginning to feel he was approaching that nicety of speed, litheness, and endurance that meant he was in top shape.

It was after one of these morning workouts in late April that Hawker returned to his second-floor apartment in the Irish section of Chicago to find he had a visitor.

He knew who it was before he even went inside.

The beige Mercedes 450-SL outside told him who it was: Andrea Marie Flischmann, his ex-wife.

Ex-wife but still an old friend.

He'd known her since junior high school. Andrea with the silken hair, olive skin, and the fashion-model face. Andrea with the burning brown eyes that seemed to see to the very core of Hawker.

They had been opposites in every way. Hawker was the Irish jock, the tough red-haired kid who preferred to hang around with the guys. Andrea was the Jewish-American princess who excelled at academics and dabbled in art and politics.

Their marriage had been a bad risk. But for a sweet year it seemed they had it all. During the day they each followed their chosen occupations. Andrea was an art teacher at an exclusive private school; Hawker, a Chicago cop. At night they met on a field of mutual interest and affection: the bed.

In bed nothing else mattered. In bed Andrea was transformed from a prim, sarcastic intellectual into a wanton lioness.

But then the hours Hawker put in as a cop began to get to her. And the danger he faced. And the pressure of the near misses and close calls. As she put it, "I love being the wife of James Hawker, but I despise being the wife of a cop."

As the pressure built, the marriage began to wobble and stagger like an injured animal. Finally it collapsed.

They divorced amicably, still a little bit in love.

So when Hawker returned from his workout to see her sleek Mercedes outside, he was surprised but not shocked.

Toweling his face off, he trotted up the stairs and swung open the door of his apartment.

She stood by the window, looking out toward the gray haze of the Chicago skyline. She wore designer jeans and a green sweater over a pale green blouse. She was tall, and her dark hair was cut short and boyish. She was one of those rare women who seemed to become more beautiful as she aged. And though she would never have admitted it, her great beauty and searing wit were prime factors in the tremendous success of her exclusive art and antique shop, Reflections Gallery, in downtown Chicago.

Thus the new Mercedes. And a penthouse apartment. And a snobby group of jet set friends.

"Out slumming?" Hawker kidded as he came into the room. He tossed the towel onto the couch and began to remove his Nikes. It had been almost three months since he had last seen her. And, as always since the divorce, the beauty of her produced a sharp stab of regret in him.

She turned from the window, hands in pockets. "I've got an artist who wants a middle-aged jock for a model. Interested?"

There was a hollowness in the joke and an emptiness in her voice that Hawker caught immediately.

He walked toward her. "What's wrong, Andrea?"

She tried to force a smile, but then her face went slack, contorted, and suddenly she was in his arms, sobbing uncontrollably.

All she could do was repeat over and over, "Oh, James, they've murdered him, they've murdered him, they've killed my dear little brother. . . ."

THREE

It took Hawker a careful two hours of nursing and consoling to get the whole story out of her.

He held her in his arms until the bawling slowed to long sobs and shudders. Finally she turned gently away from him, rubbing a fist at her eyes, her mourning spent.

"You need someone to talk to?" Hawker asked softly.

"Yes. Yes, I do." She turned and looked up at him, her dark eyes glistening. "It's . . . funny, but when I first heard the news, you're the one I wanted most to see. You're the shoulder I wanted to lean on."

Hawker held her face in both hands and kissed her tenderly on the lips. "Both shoulders open. No waiting."

He sat her on the couch with a stiff Scotch and soda while he set the fireplace and lighted it. When the fire was crackling, he steamed himself clean in the shower and dressed himself in soft jeans, T-shirt, and an oiled wool sweater.

By the time he returned, she had gotten control of herself. And she was ready for another drink. While getting ice, he decided a month and a half of strict abstinence was enough. He indulged in a cold Tuborg.

Beer had never tasted better.

They made small talk. Hawker knew he had to let her work into it her own way.

Finally she did.

Her youngest brother's name was Jonathan. Hawker had seen him at a few family functions: a tall, gangly young man; jet-black hair worn longish; horn-rimmed glasses; an endearing air of innocence; and a fierce sense of indignation.

But Hawker knew him better by reputation. Jonathan had gone the Ivy League route. B.A. at Yale. Harvard Law School. Ninth in his class. He had returned to Chicago and worked for the D.A.'s office.

There he became known for his high moral values, his intense hatred of injustice, and the zeal with which he crusaded.

There was talk around town that he had a shot at becoming the youngest District Attorney in Chicago's long and sullied history. He knew all the right people, had all the right connections. But more importantly he was as tough as he was good. Apparently his talent and popularity were too much for the current D.A.'s ego to handle, and Jonathan was given his notice.

So Jonathan had put up his own shingle. Because of his reputation, he had no trouble getting private work. And according to Andrea the biggest job of his career came from an unlikely source: the Houston, Texas, District Attorney's office.

She sat on the floor now, her knees pulled up against her chest. The flame on the grate caught the depth of her brown eyes and the childlike texture of her skin. The Scotch and soda was molten amber in her right hand.

There was a sad and dreamy expression on her face as she talked, and Hawker interrupted as little as possible.

"I got word this morning," she began. "The D.A.'s office in Houston called. A man named Blakely. Somehow they knew my parents weren't in the best of health, so he wanted me to break the news." Her voice trembled slightly, and she went on. "I knew that Jonathan had been working down there for the last eight months, but I didn't know on what. The man from the District Attorney's office told me as delicately as he could. He seemed a little surprised that I didn't break into a million screaming pieces, and maybe it was relief on his part that made him so willing to explain to me what had happened and why. I'm sure a lot of what he told me was classified."

She sniffed and sipped at her drink, peering deep into the fire. "Nearly two years ago the Houston D.A.'s office got word of a slavery ring operating near the city. It was highly organized, yet it kept a very low profile. The slavers preyed on Mexicans who had entered, or wanted to enter, the United States illegally.

"According to the man I talked with this morning, the slaves are kept on large, isolated ranches. There are ranches in Texas, apparently, the size of small states—and run with better security. The D.A.'s office decided it would be best to bring in an outside investigator. Someone who had no ties to the area and therefore could see more clearly just how high the rot went. They hired Jonathan. He spent the last eight months working under cover, compiling hard evidence, taking testimony, and following leads. Last week Jonathan called the D.A.'s office from some little Mexican border town outside Rio Bravo. He told the D.A. he had uncovered evidence that a certain millionaire Texas rancher was not only involved in the slavery ring but had financed and equipped his own small army, which he used to acquire more land and oil rights from smaller ranchers. Jonathan told the D.A.'s office he would be sending them a four-hundred-page report within the week, complete with names, dates, incriminating documents, and eyewitness testimony."

She sighed, swirled the Scotch in her glass, and finished. "The report never arrived, James. Jonathan apparently made it back to Houston okay. They found him very early this morning. His apartment had been ransacked. The report was gone. And Jonathan had been shot. Murdered. They found him on the floor of his study." Her voice broke. "He wasn't even wearing his glasses . . . and the poor boy couldn't . . . couldn't see a thing without his glasses."

"I'm sorry, Andrea. I really am."

She looked at him, her eyes moist. "The Houston D.A. says they'll get the people who did it, James. He promised me. But he said it'll take a long time. He said the people responsible probably have a lot of money. And you know what that means."

Hawker's jaw tightened. "Yeah," he said. "I know."

"James," she went on, "I don't think I've asked you for a single thing since we've been divorced, have I?"

"No, Andrea. I'm sorry to say you haven't."

Her eyes were like those of a sad young child. "I'm asking you for something now, James. I want you to go down there. I want you to find out what happened to Jonathan . . . and *why*. I'm not looking for revenge, James. But I *am* looking for justice.

Jonathan had so much to offer . . . so much to give. It's just such a damnable . . . *waste.*"

She shuddered again, and as she did she held her arms out toward Hawker, and Hawker scooped her up, holding her through the long crying jag that followed.

So what can you say to a woman who is crying? Even when she's your ex-wife?

Nothing.

Hawker held her tenderly, stroking her hair and patting her. Finally she fell into a fitful sleep, laying there in his arms beside the fire. And then Hawker, tired by the long morning workout, also drifted off.

It seemed they awoke simultaneously. It must have still been well before noon, but the fire and the overcast sky outside made it seem later.

Hawker opened his eyes to find that he was looking deep into the liquid brown eyes of Andrea. Their noses were only inches apart, and she was smiling.

"Thanks," she whispered. "Thanks for listening."

"No charge, lady. Anytime." Hawker made a move as if to get up, but she stopped him with a touch of the hand.

"And how has your love life been, Mr. James Hawker?"

Hawker felt his abdomen stir at the fresh huskiness in her voice. It was a tone he recognized.

"My love life? Dull. Bo Derek's supposed to stop by at seven, and that Ronstadt girl—she claims to be some kind of singer—says she'll be here at eight. That means I'll have to hurry with Dolly. And believe me, it's no easy job to hurry with Dolly. . . ."

Andrea touched her finger to his lips. "I wish mine was as

dull. The last three men I've been interested in have been gay. Artists, you know."

"Geez. That must be like opening an empty box at Christmas."

"You don't have to sound so happy about it." She propped her head on one elbow and kissed him softly on the lips. Her mouth was moist and warm. Hawker cupped his hand behind her head and pulled her face to his and kissed her again. She seemed shy and tender at first, but then she groaned softly as she settled back on the carpet. Her mouth opened, wet and wanting, and her back arched.

He could feel the tension go out of her muscles when he touched her, and he knew that in some strange way this was to be a necessary release for her. A way of saying yes to life in the face of her brother's death.

Hawker's right hand slid up the rutted curvature of her ribs and found the heavy, warm weight of her breast. She groaned again and pulled him tighter to her as her own hand searched for and found the opening at the top of his jeans.

Then suddenly she was standing, her back to him. She pulled the sweater off in one fluid motion, then unbuttoned her blouse. She wore no bra, and her breasts were paler than the skin of her bare abdomen. They were full and heavy, with very long, dark nipples that strained upward.

On his knees now, Hawker unzipped her jeans and slid them down to her ankles. She stepped out of them, standing before the fire only in sheer beige panties through which he could see the black gloss of her pubic thatch.

Hawker slid the panties down as his lips traced the heat of her thighs. Andrea's fists knotted in Hawker's hair as his tongue found the inner depths of her, tasting the sweet mixture of sweat and salt as he lowered her once again to the carpet.

Her back arched, and her face grew flushed as she escaped into that timeless world of physical pleasure; a world that knew no pain or loss, only the inexorable drive to join, to complete, to rebuild and prevail.

Then, with a growl, she rolled away and pounced on top of him, her eyes feverish.

Her breasts hung heavily over his face, and he touched her nipples with his tongue.

"Your turn," she purred.

"But I'm not done with you," he protested.

"You're damn right you're not."

Her hands shook as she found the zipper on his jeans and pulled his pants off. Eagerly she took him in both small hands and guided him toward her hungry mouth.

For a time she was like an animal who was starving. And Hawker could do nothing but lay there, fighting for control as the woman both used him and gave him pleasure.

"Oh, James," she moaned as the two of them approached their third—or fourth—climax. "Oh, James. Why did we ever split up?"

Hawker stopped what he was doing for a moment and kissed her belly button. "Because," he said, trying hard not to smile, "we couldn't stay in bed twenty-four hours a day."

"We could have tried," she growled. "Why in the hell didn't we try?"

FOUR

So Hawker waited on the road in the desert night. He held the Ingram submachine gun poised at hip level.

There were about a dozen of them, running toward him in the night. One of them had a rifle, and the slugs were beginning to vector in on Hawker, gouging chunks of asphalt from the road.

He knew that to run was to die.

All that lay between the little border town and Texas was fifty miles of cactus prairie. If he didn't kill them all tonight, they would hunt him come first light. And there was no place to hide on the prairie.

Hawker pulled out the Ingram's metal stock. With the stock in, the little weapon was less than a foot long. The stock doubled the length.

He had used the Ingram many times and trusted it. Even so, the weapon had its limitations. It fired 9mm shorts at the astounding rate of twelve hundred rounds per minute—if you could feed it that quickly. The long box clip in the weapon held thirty-two rounds, and Hawker had three more clips hidden beneath the serape.

But its effective killing range was only fifty meters. So he would have to wait for them to step into his killing radius. He would have to stand helplessly by while they took potshots on the run. He would have to stand and hope the frail light of the new moon wasn't enough for them to draw a bead and pray that maybe, just maybe, they might guess him to be unarmed and try to take him alive.

But he had worked too hard, come too far, to be hunted.

It had not been an easy investigation.

That gray morning in April with Andrea had turned into twenty-four hours of love. Sometimes she was as rough and hungry as a lioness. Other times she was gentle and a little sad and would break into soft tears after their lovemaking.

She had been close to her brother. She had loved him dearly, and it was her first experience with a family death.

Hawker had enough experience with it to draw on, and he helped her through the tough moments.

They never left his apartment. They would love, fall into light sleep, then awake to shower and eat and love again. In those twenty-four hours, Hawker sensed Andrea had chosen this time as her period of mourning and her period of healing. He felt a strange pride that after all these years it was still he whom she chose to be with at her most uncertain hour.

But finally it ended. The woman dressed herself, gave him a sisterly peck on the cheek, and walked back down the stairs toward the Mercedes and the fast and glittery existence that was her world.

And Hawker remained alone. Alone with his commitment to help. Alone with his promise to track down the goons who had murdered her brother.

The first thing he did was call Jake Hayes. He didn't have to clear his vigilante plans with Hayes, but he did want to touch base. Hayes had grown up in Texas, and he would no doubt have some powerful connections that might be of use.

Hendricks, the English butler who had spent the war working under cover for Great Britain's MI-5, answered the phone.

"Hank!" Hawker had exclaimed. "Is the boss in?"

The Englishman's dry wit was like a razor. "Chubby? Is that you? Taken a break from the fats and sweets long enough to contact old friends, have we?"

Hawker laughed. "I've trimmed down to a lean one ninety-five, you mean old man. And I'm running seven-minute miles."

"My, that sort of speed *will* come in handy in a fight. The French used it quite effectively at the beginning of the war when they ran from the Germans."

Still laughing, Hawker pressed, "Now that you've called me a fat coward, can I talk to Jake?"

Hawker could imagine the stoic, sober face breaking into a grin. "Of course, dear boy. No one the two of us would rather hear from."

Jacob Hayes was immediately sympathetic as Hawker repeated Andrea's story. Of course he would provide the backing. Yes, he would help in any way he could.

"But I should warn you, James," Hayes added. "You haven't spent much time in south Texas. And I suspect it's like no place you've ever seen before. As big as it is, there's still a small-town mentality there. They're a tight-knit group. They don't like out-siders. Some of those millionaire ranchers quite literally are like feudal lords. Whole villages depend on them for survival. Their jobs, their homes, their cars—everything. And most of them run their towns with an iron fist. Because of their wealth and because of their power, the law—quite literally—doesn't apply to them. The townspeople know that, so don't be surprised if they're reluctant to help."

"I've run into walls before, Jake."

"I know that, James. And I also know that no one is better at going *through* walls than you. It's just a word of warning. Most of the people you'll find there are good people. Damn good people. If they like you. But if they don't like you . . . well, just be careful, that's all."

"I will, Jake. And you'll have my equipment delivered?"

"By a personal courier—the moment you call with an address. And I'll also have a list of men in Houston, San Antonio, and Corpus Christi you can contact if you need help. Old friends of mine."

"Great, Jacob. I'll stay in touch."

So James Hawker dropped from the canned air and non-smoking section of thirty-seven thousand feet into the steel and glass glare of Houston. Dropped from the friendly skies of United into the dry heat of the West's Big Apple with its Lone Star billboards and tooled-leather Cadillacs and its Willie Nelson savvy.

Caught a cab through the rush and glitter of the city built by cowpokes, oil barons, sheikhs, rednecks, and millionaire good ol' boys. Rented a private apartment and cabled Jake Hayes his address. Ate a surprisingly satisfying hamburger with barbecue sauce at a place called Rio Bravo Burger. Then went out for a long run to get the feel of the city.

Beneath the glitter, Houston had an atmosphere all its own. An energy of regionalism and independence. There were more western-wear shops than K-Marts. More Rio Bravo Burger franchises than McDonald's.

Hawker knew he was there for a long stay.

It took him a week just to get an appointment with the Houston D.A.—and then only through the pressure brought to bear by one of Jake Hayes's powerful friends.

The D.A. was an older, powerfully built man who wore his western three-piece suit as comfortably as the farmer he looked like might wear overalls. His name was Gas Blakely. "Gas" short for Gasteau according to the brass nameplate on his desk.

He had a hard, meaty handshake, thin blond hair, and a flushed, corpulent face that hid its weariness behind a big grin of welcome. The office was leather and fine wood, and the plush red carpet was a gigantic Navajo weave.

As Hawker took a seat, Blakely propped his expensive ostrich-skin boots on the desk and fired up a cigar. "Mr. Hawker," he began, "no one feels worse about the death of Jonathan Flischmann than I do. He was my boy. I hired him, brought him down here and turned him loose. He was my responsibility and I fucked up." He shot a plume of smoke into the air, and his expression was a mixture of anger and self-reproach. "I don't think I can put it any plainer than that."

Hawker nodded at his frankness. "As you know, I'm a friend of Jonathan's family, and they thought if I came down—"

"Let's cut the bullshit, Mr. Hawker," Blakely interrupted, swinging his feet off the desk and leaning forward. "You obviously have some powerful friends—that's how you got in here to see me. Right from your first call, I had you marked as some half-assed private eye that Jonathan's people sent down to give us slow-thinking, slow-talking good ol' boys a kick in the ass. They want to see justice done, so they hired their own man—that's the way I had it figured."

Hawker's eyes narrowed. "And how do you have it figured now, Mr. Blakely?"

The big District Attorney smiled for the first time. "You rile quick, don't you? That's the way it is with you redheads. Hell, I ought to know. I married one! And from the look in your eyes, Mr. Hawker, I wouldn't want to get on your bad side. No siree." He laughed, and for the first time Hawker realized that he wasn't getting the quick brush-off as he had thought he would.

"I'm licensed as a private investigator, but that's not why I'm here," Hawker said mildly.

The smile vanished from Blakely's face, and once again Hawker could see the weariness in the man. "I know exactly why you're here, Mr. Hawker. I've checked your background thoroughly—and a very impressive background it is. But that's not how I found out why you're here. Word of mouth, Mr. Hawker. That's how I learned. Rumors here, stories told in back rooms there. Yesterday, it suddenly dawned on me. A red-haired ex-cop. You're becoming something of a legend among the law enforcement agencies around this country. Los Angeles was your last stop, wasn't it? Or was it New York?" Blakely let the silence build for a moment before adding, "No one will speak openly about you and what you do. But the word's out just the same."

Hawker's expression didn't change. "You must be mistaking me for someone else, Mr. Blakely. Like I said—I'm just a friend of the family's."

"Right. Like Patton was a friend of the queen." The big D.A. wiped his palm across his face as if trying to wipe away the responsibilities of his position. "Do you know what really pisses me off about Jonathan's death, Mr. Hawker? What really pisses me off is that it was such a professional job. We don't have a damn thing to go on—and won't. So now we're going to have to bring in someone else to take Jonathan's position. And he's going to put in eight more months of hard work tracking these bastards down—if he lives, that is. And then we're going to spend two years in the courts trying to prosecute them and even *then* probably only end up with the small fry. And do you know why, Mr. Hawker? The reason is, we've got to follow every tiny little letter of the law. We've not only got to touch all the bases, we've got to touch them twice. And do you know what the people responsible for Jonathan's death are going to be doing while we're touching all the bases? They're going to be laughing their asses off while they hide their tracks."

"Is that the news you want me to take back to Jonathan's family, Mr. Blakely?" Hawker asked.

"Officially? You're damn right it is—because that's the way it has to be." His eyes locked onto Hawker's. "But unofficially, I almost wish you were the guy I thought you were. Because, if you were"—he reached into his drawer and slapped a thin folder onto the desk—"I'd give you this list of names. It's the same list I gave Jonathan eight and a half months ago. It was his starting point. And to uncover this slave ring and to find Jonathan's killers, a man would have to jump right back into his footprints."

"I understand Jonathan called you just before he died."

"Yes. That's right."

"Did he give you any indication who was involved in the slave ring?"

Blakely shook his head. "That's the unfortunate thing. No names. No specifics. He wanted to save all that until I read his report. But he did say one curious thing. He said that he had uncovered a hell of a lot more than just a slavery ring. He said Texas wouldn't be the same once his report came out."

"He had found something much bigger?"

"That was the implication."

"Any idea what it might be?"

Blakely shook his head. "Jonathan was smart. He played his cards pretty close to the chest. Too close in this instance." The big man smiled. "And you're asking an awful lot of questions for just a friend of the family."

As Hawker stood to leave, Gas Blakely added, "There are a few other things I'd tell this red-haired vigilante, Mr. Hawker. I'd tell him that if he needed some advice or more information to call the number on the inside leaf of that folder. It's my private line, and I have it checked once a week to make sure it's clean." Blakely stood to face him. He reached into his jacket pocket and took a large pinch of snuff from a can of Copenhagen. "And there's something else I'd tell him," he went on. "I'd tell him not to get caught, Mr. Hawker. I'd tell him not to get caught in Texas because, if he does, we'd put him in jail and throw away the key. Do you understand my meaning, Mr. Hawker?"

James Hawker reached and picked up the file. As he left the room he said, "I understand you totally, Mr. Blakely. And if I see this mysterious red-haired guy, I'll pass it along."

FIVE

So Hawker took the list of names Gas Blakely gave him and went to work.

As Jake Hayes had warned, it was not easy work.

Texans would not open up around a stranger from Chicago. And despite what Hawker told them, he still looked like an ex-pro running back or, at worst, a cop. Clothes are simply labels—labels that tell strangers who we are, what we do, what niche we fit in in the social order.

Hawker learned that in order to get anywhere in his investigation he would have to change roles as readily as a chameleon changes its colors.

Hawker's first role was that of the wealthy pseudo-cowboy. With Hayes's financial backing, the props were no problem. Big rented Cadillac with full bar and driver. Five-hundred-dollar boots and western suit. But there was no way he could pass himself off as a Texan because, as Hayes had pointed out, the nation's largest state still operated very much like a small town. Hawker didn't know the code words: the names of the friends of friends; the stories about who played quarterback for the high school state champions way back when.

The men of Houston's back-room power structure would have marked him as a fake in a minute.

So Hawker chose the role of the millionaire from Chicago who had always had a little bit of Texas in his heart. One of Hayes's friends fixed him up with passes to half a dozen exclusive men's clubs in Houston. So Hawker spent the week playing high stakes paddleball, talking big business, eating inch-thick porterhouses, and drinking aged bourbon with men who accepted him as a power structure member—but still an outsider.

Hawker surprised himself by how easily he fell into the role. His cover story was that he was putting together acreage for the western dream house his new wife had always wanted. He also let it be known that he liked the idea of getting into the cattle and oil business. To talk about it convincingly he had to read up on the language of big money: options, buy-backs, fliers, rollover investments, and a dozen other terms that took the glamour out of money and made it just another commodity, like soybeans.

Hawker had never been particularly interested in money, so it was all new to him. Oddly, he found himself amused at the realization that to enter the world of big business you didn't need money. You just needed the trappings of the current power structure—and credit.

The Texans were free with their advice about business. But to his discreet inquiries about where he could buy some dependable full-time help for the mythical ranch he was buying, he still got vague replies and empty stares.

That's when Hawker invented the one-armed ranch hand character.

He bought the serape, jeans, boots, and hat at the Salvation Army store in downtown Houston. The serape gave him the camouflage he needed for his weaponry. Even so, he had a local seamstress make him a modified chest protector to go under the serape and his western shirt. The chest protector would hide his right arm and the bulge of weapons from an unprofessional frisk. And the missing arm would make him seem harmless to the men he now hunted. After all, what was there to fear from a man with one arm?

Before he left Houston, he bought an ancient pickup truck, had a few options built for it, then tossed an equally old saddle and bags into the back and headed south with the list of contacts that the late Jonathan Flischmann had traced only nine months earlier.

It was in this role that Hawker began to make headway. He spent two weeks traveling the dusty, hot back roads seeking contacts, and finally, on a desolate stretch of State Route 16, well south of Seven Sisters, Texas, Hawker located Sancho Rigera, one of the names on the list.

Sancho was a small Mexican man with a big grin and a bigger family: five sons; seven daughters; and a chubby, overworked, but happy, wife. Sancho lived in a neat three-room adobe cottage that had a 1930 vintage telephone but no plumbing. Rigera had come to the attention of the Houston D.A.'s office when he complained that certain men were trying to force him and several others in his little village to turn over the mineral rights to his farmed-out hundred-acre ranch.

It was suspected by the D.A.'s office that these same men were involved with the slavery ring.

Hawker spent five days with the Rigeras under the guise of his truck breaking down. He helped them work around the ranch during the day, and at night he sat outside beside the adobe oven and ate tortillas and beans with the family.

They were poor but seemed content, and Hawker came to like them very much. Even so, Sancho turned a deaf ear to Hawker's questions about the men who had tried to force him to sell.

Finally he hit upon an idea. Sancho Rigera had too much pride to share his problems with a guest. But he might share them with a business partner. Hawker got the name of a corporate attorney from Gas Blakely. He had papers drawn up for a company called Chicago Fossil Fuels Ltd. He made Sancho Rigera president, and himself vice-president.

"You see, Sancho," he said one night as they sat beneath the stars with two cold bottles of Dos Equis beer. "You sell a one-year option on your property's mineral rights to our corporation. You might also speak with your neighbors and see if they wish to become a part of the corporation."

"I do not understand," said Sancho Rigera, his ever-present smile white in the light of the adobe fire. "We already own the mineral rights."

"Don't you see, Sancho? People cannot force you to turn them over if they have already been acquired by another company. These men who attacked you and threatened you will not know that you and your neighbors own the corporation."

Sancho nodded at the wisdom in that. "But what do you get from this, my friend?" he asked simply.

Hawker had smiled. "Has oil ever been found in this area?"

The little Mexican shook his head. "Never. Not to my knowledge."

"Then I will get what you get—nothing. And, if oil ever is discovered, the contract will read that as vice-president of the corporation I am entitled to a yearly salary of one dollar. Nothing more."

"That is unfair. But we will not discuss it now. It is enough that you have had this idea. It will help us, and I thank you for that. Please, allow my beautiful daughter, Juanita, to fetch us another beer from the well." The Mexican nodded and moved closer to Hawker. "There is another matter I wish to discuss with you. It is about these men you seek. These evil men who steal and sell human beings. Are you still interested in them"—his smile broadened—"or perhaps you wish to remain and search for the oil with us?"

Hawker tried not to show how very anxious he was. "Please understand that I do not think you should look for oil, Sancho. You will only waste your time. But, yes, I am still interested in these men. Do you think they are associated with the men who tried to force you into selling your mineral rights?"

Sancho used one finger to push his straw cowboy hat back. Now he whispered, "It is not a wise thing to speak of such matters to strangers, but you are no longer a stranger. We are business partners, is that not true? And now we are also friends."

Hawker accepted the beer from the pretty teenage Mexican girl and said nothing. Sancho continued. "I cannot say if the two are related. I know who harassed us for our mineral rights, and he is a man of such great wealth and power that it would be madness for us ever to think of revenge. But the slavery is another matter. It must be stopped. That is why I will tell you this thing. There is a bar beyond Rio Bravo, fifty miles south of the Mexican border. I have heard that it is the most evil place in all of Mexico. It is called the Bar of the Unknown Souls. These men you seek, these men who kidnap and sell people, you may find there. But I warn you, my friend, be careful. You have only one arm, and these are dangerous men. You must take a weapon with you. In the house I have such a thing. A shotgun with two barrels . . ."

Hawker patted the little man's shoulder fondly. "I will find my own weapon, friend Sancho. You must keep your shotgun." And the teenage girl blushed when he added, "With so many beautiful daughters around, a father may find some use for it."

Sancho Rigera nodded importantly. "Yes, this is true. Especially now that we are going into the oil business. The oil will bring us great wealth, and my daughters must be protected."

James Hawker smiled and said nothing.

The next morning he left for Mexico.

SIX

As the men from *Las Almas Desconocidas* came fanning down the dark road toward him, Hawker let the Ingram submachine gun hang by its sling as he threw up his hands.

He hoped that would stop them from firing at him. He wanted at least one of them alive, and he could only be sure of doing that if they stopped firing.

Instead his show of weakness only made them run faster and shoot more. Hawker knew what was going through their brains: The gringo was unarmed, so there was nothing to fear. And the man who killed him would probably be rewarded in some small way.

So they were all anxious for the kill.

He expected to see the fat bartender with the greasy shoulder-length hair, but he was not among the dozen men. Hawker decided that the bartender must be higher up in the organization than he had thought. More than a field soldier, anyway. But probably not much more.

The semi truck carrying the beautiful Cristoba de Abella was now little more than a speck of light on the flat empty road to Texas. As Hawker brought the Ingram up to his hip he wondered how badly she had been wounded. The slug she took might have broken her arm—at worst.

But Hawker knew that her physical wound would not compare with the emotional trauma she would suffer if he did not find her soon.

What was she? Twenty? Within a year the heroin injections and the forced sex would have her looking forty. After that, they would junk her. Abandon her on the streets to the living hell of a drug addict.

Hawker's hand grew tight on the Ingram.

Yes, he had to find her. And he had to find her soon.

In the weak light of the new moon, Hawker saw that at least three of the dozen or so men carried rifles.

When one of the rifle slugs dug the asphalt away from his feet, Hawker dropped to his belly and fired.

The first burst from the submachine gun cut the legs from beneath his first four attackers. The chain-rattle clatter of the Ingram echoed in Hawker's ears, mingling with the fresh screams of agony.

The sharp odor of gunpowder replaced the sagelike odor of cactus and mesquite.

Two of the men writhed in agony on the asphalt forty yards away. The other two lay still. Deathly still.

About half of the men who remained turned and ran back toward the bar. Hawker jumped to his feet to pursue them, but an immediate volley of small-weapons fire put him back on his belly.

Not all of them were cowards. Some of them had chosen to stay and fight.

Hawker wondered how many of them remained.

There was a ditch beside the road, and Hawker rolled into it. His attackers were on the west side of the road. Hawker lay in the ditch on the east.

He began to work his way down the ditch, staying low. He guessed that most of them had retreated fifteen to twenty yards—so that meant they were just under a hundred yards away.

It crossed Hawker's mind that if he could work his way past them, he could sneak back to the sleazy bar and beat some information out of the bartender and leave without another confrontation.

That seemed like the wisest plan. But then Hawker remembered the look of terror on the face of the girl and the others chained inside the truck.

No, these men who now tried to kill him deserved a confrontation. And they damn well deserved to die.

Hawker pulled a fresh clip from beneath the serape and held it in his left hand so he could re-arm the Ingram just as quickly as possible.

He crawled through the ditch for what seemed a very long time. All was quiet save for the agonized groan of one of the men he had shot, and the haunting wail of a coyote.

When Hawker judged he was almost directly across from his attackers, he drew himself slowly to one knee and looked across the road.

A voice from behind stopped him in his tracks. *"Freeze, gringo. Drop your weapon!"*

Hawker did not hesitate. He dove to his left as pistol fire plowed the earth behind him. He brought the Ingram up and held it on full fire, spraying in the direction from which he had heard the heavy Spanish voice.

The man had been standing. He was a squat silhouette against the desert sky. The 9mm slugs smacked through his body, contorting him into a hundred different positions like some weird cartoon character slapping ants.

When Hawker released the trigger, the man fell heavily into the sand, as if he had fallen from a table. His leg quivered, and then he lay still.

Voices from across the road yelled hopefully, "Orlando—is the gringo dead? Did you kill him?"

Hawker punched the empty clip out and slid a fresh thirty-two rounds into the Ingram. The metal barrel was hot against his hands.

When Orlando did not answer, Hawker could hear them whispering nervously among themselves. He wished his Spanish were better. After a long pause he heard the heavy crunch of men running. For a moment he thought they were running away.

But then he realized they were charging him.

The moment Hawker poked his head up above the ditch, they opened fire. There were four of them. Their handguns belched fire in a deafening volley. Hawker flattened himself against the sand and squeezed the trigger. The Ingram was like a living creature in his hands, lunging and jolting as if to escape.

But for the men who charged him, there was no escape. Even in the darkness Hawker could see them fold and tumble backward, as if hit all at once by some gigantic club.

A moment later there was an eerie silence, broken only by the heated ticking of the Ingram.

Hawker got quickly to his feet. Carefully he approached the bodies and checked them one by one.

Dead. All dead.

Hawker listened carefully for the distant sound of a siren. He heard nothing.

Obviously, the men who operated from the bar had more to lose than to gain from calling the Mexican police.

Something they had hidden away in the bar?

Hawker wondered.

He punched out the empty clip and slid in his last fresh load.

He adjusted the serape and his hat, then headed off at a steady jog for the dim lights of the Bar of the Unknown Souls.

How long had it been since the slavers' truck had pulled away from the bar?

Half an hour? Maybe longer.

However long, it was enough time for the fat bartender to chase away his customers and lock the doors.

The gravel parking lot was nearly empty. But the weary neon light still advertised *Las Almas Desconocidas* over the doorway. Hawker tested the door, then banged on it with his fist.

Immediately he jumped back—and just in time. Slugs punched through the door as the muffled sputter of an automatic weapon roared from inside.

Hawker tried to give the scream the right pitch of terror and desperation: *"I'm shot. Shit! Get a doctor, somebody, please...."*

The moment the door cracked open, Hawker stuck his foot in it, then yanked it wide with his left hand.

The guy inside had an old Thompson. Hawker had used and admired the World War II classic, but it had its drawbacks. It was too long and heavy for close work, and now Hawker was thankful.

It took the man a long, awkward moment to get the Thompson up to fire. Hawker grabbed the barrel, swung it away, and, at the same moment, clubbed the man in the face with the butt of the Ingram.

The man—a husky black man—back pedaled against the wall, then charged Hawker, hitting him waist-high. Hawker kneed him in the chest. When the black man jolted backward, Hawker cracked him hard on the temple with his left elbow.

The blow sent him to the floor. Hawker was immediately on him, his nose only inches from the nose of the black man.

"Where is he?" Hawker hissed. "Where's the fat bartender?"

The man's eyes were glazed and slightly crossed from the beating he had just taken. "Back room," he whispered. His head motioned beyond the bar.

"Is he alone?"

The man hesitated just long enough for Hawker to know it was a lie. "Yes," he said. "Hernando is alone, yes."

As Hawker stood, the black man made a quick motion toward the Thompson, which lay just out of his reach. Hawker swung the Ingram toward his face. "Go ahead," he whispered. "If you're really feeling lucky." He kicked the Thompson toward him.

The man shook his head quickly, as if he were being wrongly accused. But the moment Hawker turned his back, he heard the quick scrape of metal. Hawker whirled and squeezed off two quick shots.

The black man's head exploded, and the Thompson was thrown against the wall as his arms convulsed upward.

"Bad choice," Hawker whispered.

Most of the lights in the bar had been switched off. The place stank of cigarette smoke and stale beer. Hawker noticed that the table on the stage had not been removed.

Hawker knew that the mirror behind the bar was a two-way mirror. He pretended to ignore it.

He walked softly, carefully, his ears tuned for any noise.

From some unknown source there came a muted, metallic *click*.

The sound registered immediately: It was the noise of a shot-gun being snapped closed.

Hawker dropped instantly to his belly. As he did there was a deafening roar, and the mirror jumped outward, away from the bar. Glass rained down on Hawker.

On his knees, he crawled quickly to the end of the bar and popped up, the Ingram vectoring. A head materialized behind the row of liquor bottles where the mirror had once been. For a microsecond Hawker had the strange impression he was at a shooting gallery.

He squeezed off a shattering burst of fire. The 9mm slugs tore through the man in the next room, spinning him around. In the same instant another man jumped up, and an automatic pistol threw a flame toward Hawker's head. There was a sudden vacuum of air near Hawker's ear, which told him the slug had narrowly missed him.

The man never got the chance to try a second time. Hawker held the Ingram on steady burst, and the man was thrown into oblivion, his face drenched with gore.

Hawker swung around the bar and hesitated by the door, listening. He sensed more than heard that someone stood just beyond, waiting for him. Holding the submachine gun at hip level, the vigilante shot through the door, then kicked the door open. As he entered, the heavy shadow of the fat bartender disappeared down the hall. Hawker turned the Ingram to squeeze off a quick shot—but the weapon clicked empty.

Hawker cursed himself softly for not carrying more ammunition. But he had come expecting trouble—not a war.

Quickly he bent over one of the corpses. It was the man with the little automatic pistol. A Walther PPK with a stainless body.

Not a cheap weapon.

Hanker wondered who was financing them.

As he tried to pry it from the dead man's hands, a deep voice laughed. "So the one-armed gringo is really a two-armed cop?" The laughter thickened. "And now he is out of bullets. And now he is going to die."

Hawker turned to see the fat bartender, Hernando, his greasy hair like a towel over his shoulders. He was holding a Winchester 97 12-gauge pump gun leveled at Hawker's face.

The bartender walked toward him, stopping so the barrel of the Winchester was just out of Hawker's reach. "You have killed many men tonight, gringo. Many of my best men. You have caused me great inconvenience. Our Mexican police are not as fussy about details as you Americano cops—but even so, it will not be easy explaining so many dead bodies to them."

Hawker stood easily on the balls of his feet. He took two slow steps backward, hoping it would bring the fat bartender closer to him.

It did.

"Kill me if you want to," Hawker said easily. "But don't kill me as a cop. I'm down here because a friend of mine was murdered. A man named Jonathan Flischmann. Know anything about it?"

The Mexican's grin never left his face. "I know that he was a lawyer, and like all lawyers he asked too many questions. I know that he was a threat to my employer." His grin broadened. "I did not know that he had been killed. But now that I know, I am glad."

"Yeah," said Hawker, taking another step backward. "I guess he found out about your rich Texan boss, huh? About how he uses this bar as a front for a slave ring. Right now some other friends of mine are following that slave truck of yours into Texas. And when it gets to its destination, everyone involved is going to be arrested."

Hernando gave a noncommittal shrug. "Is that so? Then I am surprised you did not run when you had the chance."

As the bartender took another half-step toward him, Hawker faked an arcing overhand right at the Mexican's face, then dropped to his knees as the shotgun gouged a hole in the wall behind him. As he dropped, Hawker's hand disappeared beneath his serape, and then he was driving upward; upward with all his strength, driving the seven-and-a-half-inch blade of his Randall Attack/Survival knife deep into the fat Mexican's groin.

The Randall Model 18, with its hand-sharpened carbon-steel body and saw-toothed upper blade slid through the flesh and gristle, then ripped its way out when Hawker jerked away.

The Mexican screamed terribly, his legs slashing in agony. Hawker pounced on him immediately, holding the knife at his throat. "Tell me," he yelled. "Tell me the name of your partner in Texas. Tell me, and I'll get you a doctor."

The fat bartender gave Hawker a burning look of fear and desperation. "Sister . . . Sister Star Ranch. Will . . . Williams. *Oh, the pain!*"

Hawker stood up quickly, his head swinging back and forth in search of a phone. He had promised the man a doctor—and he would try to get him one.

But he wouldn't stick around to help.

There was a side door off the back office, and Hawker opened it and switched on the light.

The woman who had appeared on stage earlier lay naked upon a bed. The blond wig she wore sat crookedly on her head. Her eyes sagged open for a moment, trying to focus on Hawker.

"Is it time?" she moaned. "Do I have to go back on already, Hernando? Give me a fix, or I won't be able to. Please, just one more, and I'll go, Hernando. I promise."

There was a telephone on the desk beside the bed. Hawker studied it for a moment. Thinking suddenly about Cristoba de Abella, the beautiful Indian girl, Hawker looked at the pathetic woman on the bed. "How did you get here?" he asked. "Where are you from?"

The woman stared at him, incoherent. "Why, *you* brought me here, Hernando. Don't you remember? I was on vacation and I trusted you, and *you* brought me here."

The woman settled back on the bed in what she thought was a suggestive pose. She rubbed her hands over the stretch-mark-scarred breasts and licked her lips. "If you make me a fix, I'll give you something nice in return, eh? Something real nice, okay?"

Feeling an involuntary nausea, Hawker switched out the light and closed the door behind him. Hernando, still writhing in agony, looked up at him expectantly.

Hawker picked up the empty Ingram and slung it over his shoulder. "Bad news, Hernando," Hawker said as he headed toward the bar's front door. "You're going to have to make your own phone call—even if it means you'll never trust me again."

SEVEN

It took Hawker only a few hours to get back across the border.

He jettisoned all weaponry but the handmade Randall knife. He doubted if news of the mass killings had reached the border guards yet, but he wanted to take no chance of his weapons being found.

But once he got back into Texas, he could not afford to hurry. He needed more information. He needed specifics.

Twenty-four hours later, from a phone booth in Weslaco, he called Gasteau Blakely. Blakely was not pleased, to say the least.

"Jesus Christ, Hawker!" he yelled. "What went on down there in Mexico last night?"

"I have no idea what you're talking about, Gas," Hawker answered calmly. "I spent a couple of days playing tourist. Bought a basket. People down there were real friendly. Quite a welcome I got at one bar in particular—"

"What about the welcome *you* gave, for God's sake! Shit, Hawker, I thought those rumors I'd heard about you had been exaggerated. Hell, you're a damn war machine—"

"Hang on, Gas. Like I said, I have no idea what you're talking about. But if this guy is all he's supposed to be, then you can bet the guys who got hit down there damn well deserved to get hit. But that's not why I'm calling. I'm calling because I need information. There's the name of a man I want you to check on, and the name of a ranch. . . ."

Finally Blakely calmed down enough to promise he would check out both for Hawker. But he finished with a warning. "Damn it, Hawker, I don't want that shit going on in my district. Do you hear me? If you go one step over the line in my district, I'm going to put your ass in jail and feed the key to the hogs."

"Nice talking to you, too, Gas," Hawker said, smiling. "And like I said: I don't know what in the hell you're talking about."

So Hawker stuck to the back roads, bouncing along in the battered Chevy pickup truck. He stopped at desolate ranches, small towns, and two gas stations.

He talked with people. He ate and drank with them. He asked questions about the Bar of the Unknown Souls and about rumors of a slavery ring. Always the reaction was the same. These good, friendly people turned inward, uncommunicative. He was welcome as a man, but his questions were not wanted. The impression Hawker had of this organization was now doubly strong: It was a source of terror to all who had heard of it.

So Hawker would ask his questions and move on. Once again he was the one-armed drifter. Once again he was on the trail.

But now he had something to go on. The name of a ranch: The Sister Star. And the name of a man: Williams.

Every night he stopped at a ranch house and traded work for a place to sleep in the barn. And every night he drove to the nearest town and tried to call his second connection: Sancho Rigera. And always there was no answer, or he got a recording saying the phone was out of order.

Just when Hawker decided he should drive back to Sancho's ranch and make sure he and his family were all right, the little Mexican finally answered.

It had been nearly two weeks since they had talked, and Sancho seemed delighted to hear from him. "My friend and partner, it is so good of you to call. I was just telling the *esposa* that I feared the bad men had taken you."

"And I was beginning to think the same about you, Sancho. I couldn't get you on the phone."

"Hah! This telephone. This dirty machine!" Hawker heard him spit in contempt. "There is a devil inside this *teléfono* sent to vex me. It breaks. I ride twenty miles to contact the telephone company. But when the men arrive two days later to fix it, it is no longer broken. The men look at me as if I am crazy. And then, the moment they leave, it refuses to work once again. A curse on this instrument!"

Hawker laughed at the little man's anger. "I called because I need some information, Sancho. There's a ranch named—"

"I will help you in any way I can, my friend," the little man cut in. "But first I have some things to discuss. Some matters of business," he added importantly. "The documents of our corporation arrived three days ago. My neighbors, the silly men, found it impossible to believe that I was president of a company as important as Chicago Fossil Fuels Limited. Can you imagine their surprise when I showed them these documents? It was a moment of such importance that we toasted it with mescal.

Whenever another neighbor arrived, we toasted it again. Soon there was a party."

"Did the documents survive?" Hawker asked wryly.

"But of course. Juan Probisco, the nasty man, stained them with oil from his hands. I was very angry, James, but then Juan suggested that it might be a good thing—the stain of oil on the documents of a company that seeks oil."

"Yes, indeed." Hawker smiled. "A good omen."

"It was a good omen for Juan, because I was about to smack him with a hammer."

"Sancho," Hawker pressed, "I need to ask you about a certain ranch—"

"Yes, but first the news!" the Mexican interrupted. "I was about to tell you: We have selected a spot to dig for oil!"

"Sancho, you don't understand. We didn't form that company to actually look for oil. We formed that company so that you and your neighbors wouldn't be harassed anymore."

The hurt in Sancho's voice was plain. "But what is the use of being president of such a company if the company does not actually seek oil? At this party of which I spoke, all of my neighbors signed this fine document, James. We are all members now. And while it is true you are vice-president, I am still the *president*—"

"Okay, okay, Sancho, we'll look for oil," Hawker said, chuckling. "And you've already picked the spot?"

"We have," Sancho Rigera said with authority. "It was my friend Juan's idea. It was reasoned this way: If a man seeks gold in a river, what must he first do? He must first put a little gold in that river. Do you see? Gold attracts gold. It is Juan's understanding that it is the same with all things of value: silver, diamonds . . . *and oil.*"

"It makes sense so far," Hawker said agreeably. "Sure."

"Does it not? That is why we have such high hopes. You see, it is this way. There is a spot near our village where the women dump their bad grease. Since I was a little boy, the women of the village have always used this spot. For a hundred years, maybe more, it has been this way. It is true that this spot is not such a nice place for the nose. But what in reality is old grease?"

"Oil?" Hawker put in helpfully.

"Exactly! It is there we will dig our well. There is an old man in our village who once worked in the drilling business. It was long ago, and he learned to drill for water, not oil—but is not all drilling much the same?"

"It is, yes, indeed," Hawker said, now trying hard not to laugh. "And I wish you luck, Sancho. But now you must tell me what I wish to know."

"Of course, my friend. Anything for a partner in my business."

"Good. There is a place called the Sister Star Ranch. It's someplace in Texas, but people are reluctant to tell me about it for some reason. Do you know of it?"

The silence on Sancho's end was so long that for a moment Hawker thought his phone had gone dead again. But finally he said, "Yes, my friend. I know of it."

"Then tell me where it is, Sancho."

Hawker could tell that it pained the little Mexican to speak. "The Sister Star Ranch is in the county between LaSalle and Webb, about sixty miles west of our village. The ranch is so large that it is really a county unto itself. Star County. There are several smaller ranches on it, but they are all owned by the same man."

Hawker pressed the phone hard against his ear, straining to hear a name he already knew. "And what is this man's name, Sancho?"

"My friend," the man pleaded, "you must not go to this place. For if you do, it is certain death. Please, come live with us. You are a lonely man and homeless—but my prettiest daughter, Juanita, looks upon you favorably even though you have but one arm—"

"The man's name, Sancho. What is it?"

"His name . . . his name is Skate Williams. It was this same man whose employees tried to force us into selling our oil rights." He sighed unhappily. "And God forgive me, James, for ever telling you, for now your death is on my hands. . . ."

EIGHT

Sancho was right about the size of the Sister Star Ranch. It was a county unto itself. Almost a country unto itself.

Hawker rattled along through the rolling range of mesquite and prickly pear cactus, through the one-gas-station towns with their solitary COKE signs and peeling clapboard houses, past the rank longhorn cattle of south Texas.

At a general store outside Tilden on Highway 72, Hawker stopped for fuel and something to eat.

He wasn't really hungry. Back in Houston, he had re-armed, bathed, changed clothes, and eaten enough Rio Bravo Burgers to last him a week. But he wanted to see how people outside Star County felt about Skate Williams and his Sister Star Ranch operation.

Hawker had decided to stay with the one-armed drifter character. Back in Mexico, the only member of the organization who had survived his assault was the driver of the slave truck. And the driver had not seen him.

So he smoothed the serape and went inside the little general store. The man behind the wooden counter was a wizened, sour old man with white hair and a gigantic chaw of tobacco in his cheek. Hawker drank a quart of buttermilk and ate pig's knuckles and crackers while he tried in engage the man in conversation.

Yes, the old man said, Hawker might be able to find work in Star County. No, he didn't think it would be at Skate Williams's ranch. Skate Williams never hired. (This was said with a private smile that told Hawker just what he wanted to know.) Yes, he knew Skate Williams, and he thought he was a self-important son of a bitch.

It took Hawker nearly a full hour to dig this information out of the old man. But it was worth it. Hawker needed to know if the locals in the adjoining counties were for or against the slave lord. And if the store owner was any indication, Hawker might be able to find some backup help if he needed it.

The scenery began to change when he entered Star County. The roadside shanties disappeared, as did the dilapidated little towns. In Star County all seemed clean and undeveloped. There were miles of open range on which cattle grazed. The brand on the cattle was plain, even from the road: two overlapping stars.

Hawker saw the first of Skate Williams's ranches from about ten miles away. It was in a shallow valley by a river that rolled down out of the hills. There was a large main house and several smaller houses. As Hawker drew nearer, he could see the main house was built of stone. The barn and the outbuildings were clapboard or board and batten, painted white. Miles of five-plank fence, also painted white, rolled along the edge of the ranch.

The front gate was open, but Hawker stopped, anyway. A sign read:

SISTER STAR RANCH #4
SKATE WILLIAMS, OWNER
ROY DALTON, MGR.
ABSOLUTELY NO TRESPASSING

From the sign Hawker made two general deductions: one, Williams owned at least four such ranches, and Cristoba de Abella could be on any of them—if she was still alive; and two, Skate Williams—if his ego matched his wealth—probably didn't live here. He would live on Ranch #1.

Ignoring the sign's warning, Hawker drove through the gate and down the long drive.

The greeting he received was something less than friendly. As he pulled into the main house's circular drive, four burly men strode out to confront him. They wore old jeans, stained western shirts, and high-crowned western hats. They looked like prop toughs in some mid-forties cowboy movie.

As Hawker stepped out of the truck, the four men fanned out around the door, blocking Hawker's exit.

"You got business here?" the heaviest of them, a florid-faced man with massive hands, asked.

"Maybe," said Hawker. "I'm looking for work."

"Then maybe you telephoned ahead and got permission to apply?" the florid-faced man pressed. Hawker noted that his huge silver belt buckle read, "Jeb." Jeb wore a Ruger Blackhawk .44 in a holster strapped to his hip.

"Didn't call," Hawker said. "Didn't know I was supposed to."

As Hawker turned to slide past the men, Jeb grabbed his shoulder and swung him around. "We're talking to you, mister. Don't go trying to sneak off like that."

"Shit, Jeb," one of the other men cut in, "he ain't got but one arm."

Jeb's lips curled back. Hawker guessed it was his version of a grin. "And just what kind of work do you think a one-armed man can do around here?" He looked at the other man and winked. "We got a vet that does all our artificial insemination." He winked again. "And that's about all a one-armed man is good for, isn't it? Jackin' off bulls, and whatever other creatures that gets in his way."

The others laughed. Hawker could feel the muscles in his face grow tight. "You seem to know all about it, Jeb," Hawker said softly. "I guess it's true what Texas women say about you guys with great big belt buckles."

The big cowboy's face grew serious for a moment. "Yeah? And what do they say?"

"They say you've got tiny little dicks, Jeb. And I guess that would make you real *handy.*"

The others roared with laughter.

But Jeb didn't. He shoved Hawker roughly against the truck and threw a ponderous right fist at Hawker's face.

Hawker ducked under the punch and drove his left hand deep into the big man's solar plexus, then put all his weight behind a backhand that sent the cowboy backpedaling across the drive.

The punch to the belly had knocked most of the wind out of him, so he wheezed as he said, "You one-armed son of a bitch, I'll *kill* you for that."

Hawker could do nothing but stand helplessly as Jeb drew the Blackhawk .44—one of the most powerful sidearms ever sold.

There was the sound of a hammer clicking back—and Hawker was surprised to realize that one of the other ranch hands had also drawn a weapon. He was a tall rugged-looking man with smooth, weathered skin and bright blue eyes. The way he leveled his Colt revolver at Jeb reminded Hawker just a little bit of Gary Cooper.

"You got no call to shoot this man, Jeb," the cowboy drawled easily. "Unless you're afraid to take on a one-armed man in a fair fight."

Jeb's eyes burned as he glared at the man. "You put that side-arm away right now, Quirt Evans, or I'll shove that son of a bitch up your ass!"

The tall man he had called Quirt Evans smiled broadly. "One fight at a time, Jeb. One fight at a time." He nodded at Hawker. "Right now it looks like you got your hands full with this old boy."

Jeb glared at him for a moment more, then reluctantly holstered the Blackhawk .44. More cautiously now, he began to stalk Hawker, both fists clenched.

Hawker nodded at Evans. "Thanks," he said.

Quirt Evans winked briefly. "You can thank me later—if you live."

Hawker chuckled as he took two careful steps toward the huge cowboy. "Thanks for the reassurance," he said.

Jeb threw a series of roundhouse lefts and rights, and Hawker ducked under them all, backing away. He felt a great temptation to pull his right arm from beneath the serape and beat the hell out of this overweight bully. But if he did so, he knew he would immediately expose himself as a fraud, and all the long weeks of work would be wasted.

No, he had to fight this man—and he had to beat him using only one arm. That meant he had to stick and move; beat him with speed and skill. And under no circumstances could he allow Jeb to get him on the ground. The man was big and slow, but he looked strong as hell. On the ground Jeb would tear him apart.

Hawker allowed Jeb to come charging at him once again, still backing away. Then, at the last microsecond, he faked a high overhand left. When Jeb's hands flew up to protect his face, Hawker spun and kicked him full force in the ribs with the heel of his boot.

Jeb bowed over, sputtering. Hawker was immediately on him, cracking the florid face open with a series of left uppercuts and hooks. Jeb kept backing away, trying to get his hands up to shield his face. When his hands came up, Hawker went to work on the broad belly, putting all of his two hundred pounds behind the punches.

The huge cowboy was wobbly now, and once again he reached for his gun. But Hawker beat him to it, drawing it out of the holster and tossing it across the drive.

"I'll kill you for this," Jeb wheezed.

Hawker slapped him twice in the face, hard. "You'll what?"

"I'll kill you—"

Hawker hit him flush on the nose. His nose flattened, immediately went pale white, then began to pour blood.

"That's the second time you've said that, and both times you've been on your ass."

Hawker knew that one more good shot would put him down, but as he drew back his fist a voice stopped him.

"What in the hell is going on here?"

Hawker turned to see a lean, middle-aged man with a black mustache standing on the porch of the big house. He wore a blue western leisure suit, and a cigarette hung from the corner of his mouth.

"Jeb was just provin' to this stranger that a one-armed man ain't worth a shit." Quirt Evans laughed.

Jeb was hanging on to the wooden fence, trying hard not to fall. His face and shirt were soaked with blood, and he looked as if he were about to vomit.

The man on the porch looked from Hawker to Jeb, and then back to Hawker. "You got any particular reason for being on Sister Star property, mister?"

"Looking for work," Hawker said, trying to shake some of the pain out of his left hand. "Saw the ranch and just stopped by."

The man stepped down off the porch and stopped at a point midway between Hawker and the bloodied cowboy. He looked pointedly at Jeb. "That big mouth of yours finally got you into trouble, huh, Jeb?" He dropped his cigarette in the sand and ground it out with his foot. "Go to the bunkhouse and get cleaned up. I always had the feeling you were nothing but mouth and pussy. Pack your gear while you're at it, and get the hell off this ranch."

Jeb straightened immediately. "Hell, Mr. Dalton, I got bills to pay. I just bought me that new truck, and that Appaloosa roper ain't paid for yet—"

"I don't give a goddamn about your financial problems, Jeb. I told you to get, and I mean just that—"

"Maybe you ought to check with Mr. Williams before you go firing an old hand, Mr. Dalton," Jeb said in a tone that clearly had a double meaning. "With what I know about this operation, he might not be in such a hurry to cut me loose."

The man Hawker assumed to be Roy Dalton, the ranch manager, took a step toward the huge cowboy. His voice was calm, but there was a deadly undercurrent in his tone. "Remember what I said about that big mouth of yours, Jeb. And that busted nose ain't nothing compared to the kind of trouble we can give you."

Jeb's manner changed immediately. Hawker knew raw fear when he saw it, and that is exactly what the cowboy's face now showed. "I'm . . . I'm sorry, Mr. Dalton. I shouldn't have said what I did. I wasn't thinkin'. I'll get my stuff. I'll clear out. I got no grudges against you or Mr. Williams."

Roy Dalton stared at him and said nothing. After a moment of the ranch manager's withering silence, Jeb turned and walked quickly toward the long wooden bunkhouse.

When he disappeared through the door, Dalton turned to Hawker. "We're not hiring right now, mister," he said. "And do yourself a favor. Never step on Sister Star property again uninvited. Not all of these boys are as soft as Jeb there."

"Any kind of work's okay with me, Mr. Dalton," Hawker said quickly. "I'm reliable. I don't drink much. And if Jeb there is leaving—"

Dalton's eyes studied him carefully. Hawker felt as if he were a steer or a quarter horse being sized up. "What's your name?"

Hawker told him.

"Where are you from?"

"Around. I was born in Chicago, but I've been down in Mexico for a while."

Dalton nodded and said nothing. "You got trouble with the law?"

Hawker sensed that Dalton hoped he had. He took a chance. "Some. Nothing serious. I'm no thief. You don't have to worry about that."

Dalton nodded again, and Hawker knew that the lie had paid off. Dalton said, "Jeb there had his bad points, but he was a good man with a rope. You done much wrangling?"

Hawker knew that cowboy experience was something he couldn't lie about. These men were pros, and they would find him out in a minute. He said, "To tell you the truth, I ain't worth a damn on a horse, Mr. Dalton. I need the work, but I can't steer you wrong there."

Behind him, the other men laughed. Quirt Evans put in, "Weren't you saying something the other day about needing a cook, Mr. Dalton? That Vietnamese boy you got now can't make nothing that ain't got roots and noodles and shit in it." The other men laughed again, agreeing.

Dalton lighted another cigarette. "What about it, Hawker? Can you cook?"

"When a man loses an arm, Mr. Dalton, cooking's the second thing he learns how to do."

Dalton eyed him narrowly. "Yeah? What's the first?"

"Fight."

Dalton turned and walked away. Over his shoulder he said, "Quirt will show you where to bunk, Hawker. We eat breakfast here at five A.M. sharp. The Vietnamese boy will show you around the kitchen." He stopped suddenly and looked at Hawker. "And one more thing: We don't like trouble around here. But when we do have trouble, we take care of it ourselves. Jeb there got off easy. Usually we just kill troublemakers and feed them to the dogs."

The other men didn't laugh this time.

And Hawker knew Roy Dalton wasn't kidding.

NINE

For the first three days Hawker kept a low profile. He kept his ears open and said little.

In those three days he neither saw Skate Williams nor picked up any clues to the whereabouts of Cristoba de Abella.

But he did learn a good deal about the operation of the ranch. Skate Williams owned one of the largest farm/oil operations in the world. His Texas spread consisted of eighty square miles of land—more than fifty thousand acres.

On the property were six ranches—not four as he had first guessed. Ranch #4 where Hawker worked was exclusively a cattle ranch. It seemed to explain the near absence of Mexican slave laborers.

But three of the ranches were operated as a millet and hygear farm; a cotton farm; and one that apparently was some kind of experimental station to test exotic crops that Williams hoped to someday grow commercially. On these farms Hawker was sure he would find the slaves.

The fifth ranch was the center of the oil operation. And

Ranch #1, as Hawker had suspected, was Skate Williams's home. From the talk Hawker heard around the bunkhouse Ranch #1 had every conceivable modern nicety, including a fully equipped airport for his helicopters and Learjets, an indoor Olympic-size swimming pool, and a private rodeo stadium.

Reading between the lines and the smirks, Hawker also gathered that Williams had his own small army dedicated to more than just internal security. It seemed that Williams was a zealot on the subject of the inevitable collapse of world society. And when the collapse came, according to some of the cowboys in the bunk-house, Williams was not only prepared to defend himself but also to take control and rebuild as well.

They treated it like some kind of joke, but from what Hawker heard, Williams had collected enough armaments to qualify as a world nation. Not only that, he had sufficient natural resources on his own property to make such a wild notion actually feasible. He had grain, meat, water, and oil.

These resources were the platforms of near-monopolies that Williams controlled. A chain of gas stations. A chain of feed stores. And, with the beef, the Rio Bravo Burger franchises that Hawker had grown so fond of in Houston.

Hawker also learned that there were three kinds of employees in the Sister Star orbit: the field help; the outsiders; and, finally, the insiders.

The source of the field help was obvious—but only to Hawker. The cowboys assumed they were mostly wetbacks, content to be fed and housed by their employer.

Only Hawker seemed to know that they were actually slaves. And suddenly it made sense. Considering the private nature of Williams's passion—arming himself for the final world war and the chaos that would follow—only slaves could be trusted to work around the place. Only slaves could be depended on to stay, live, work, and die within the narrow confines of the ranch.

Hawker was relieved to realize that the wranglers in the bunkhouse were outsiders—nothing more than trusted hired help. They were paid for their special skills but not allowed into the inner sanctum. What they knew of Williams's strange operation they learned from what they heard and what they saw.

Hawker was relieved because he liked the men he worked with—especially Quirt Evans, the rangy cowboy who had stopped Jeb from shooting him that very first day.

Even so, Hawker never let his guard down. Skate Williams was obviously a brilliant organizer, and certainly no fool. Hawker remembered all too well how the plant on the slave truck had almost gotten him killed.

He trusted no one.

On the fourth night Hawker decided it was time for a surveillance mission. His better judgment told him he should wait longer before venturing out, but the memory of how he had promised Cristoba de Abella his protection was too strong.

He had to find her, and he had to find her soon. If another week went by she might be hopelessly hooked on the drugs they were pouring into her—if she wasn't hooked already.

It was a Friday night—the other ranch hands' night off. Hawker finished his chores in the kitchen, instructed the Vietnamese man to finish the cleaning, and headed toward the bunkhouse.

The bunkhouse was a long, low building with a wooden

floor. Army-type bunks were alternated from wall to wall with gray lockers. There were two doors, and mounted over each was a set of steer horns.

Hawker's bunk was at the far end, away from the community showers. From the first, his disguise as a one-armed man had made it necessary to bathe and change clothes only when the bunkhouse was empty.

It was not empty now.

Quirt Evans was lying on his bunk. He wore jeans, and his boots were covered with red dust. When Hawker came in, he looked up from the magazine he was reading: *Western Horseman.*

"All done for the night, Hawk?" Evans placed the magazine on his chest. His hat and gun belt hung on a wooden peg above his bed. "You ain't half-bad in the kitchen, boy. Chow's been pretty good since you got here."

Hawker smiled. All he had actually done in the kitchen was stop the Vietnamese cook, Chang Du, from using bean sprouts.

"Thanks, Quirt. To tell you the truth, I really hadn't done much cooking before I got here."

The lanky man laughed. "I know."

There was something about the way he said it that made Hawker uncomfortable. "Yeah? You a mind reader or something?"

Evans laughed again and laid back on his bunk with the magazine. "Maybe, Hawk. You never know."

Hawker made a show of going through his duffel, as if seeking clean clothes. Actually he had hoped to shower before heading out. Now he couldn't.

"The other boys went into town for a beer," Quirt Evans said. "Want to go?"

Hawker shook his head. He smiled. "Naw. I'm just going to get into my pickup truck and drive. Do me good to get away for a while."

Evans raised his eyebrows, peering over the magazine. "Just make sure you don't get lost and end up over at Skate Williams's place. Ol' Skate doesn't take kindly to surprise visitors."

"You know him?"

"Talked to the man maybe twice; seen him less than a dozen times. I used to ride the rodeo. Won a fair share of belt buckles, and he invited me down to one of his private rodeos. Ol' Skate musta liked something I did, 'cause he singled me out and offered me either one of two jobs. The one I chose was this one: sometimes trail boss, sometimes cow hunter." He folded the magazine, and the light from the overhead lamp glistened off the craggy face and blue eyes. "My ma died when I was twelve, and I never did know my pa. He was supposed to be some kind of millionaire oil man from Dallas. If he was, we never saw any of it—the money, I mean. So, what with following the rodeo, I never did have a place to really call home." He shrugged and smiled. "So this kind of suits me fine."

"What was the other job he offered you, Quirt?"

The smile broadened. "Sheriff of Star County."

"So Williams really does own the county?"

"Lock, stock, and flush toilet. That's why I told you not to get caught on his place." His eyes grew shrewd. "Of course, in a jaw-to-jaw between you and Skate's army, I'm not sure who I'd bet on."

Once again Hawker had the impression that Quirt Evans was toying with him, suggesting he knew a hell of a lot more than he'd come right out and say. For a moment Hawker considered telling him to lay it on the line. But then he decided it was no time for a confrontation; however unlikely it seemed to Hawker, there was a chance that Evans was one of Skate Williams's plants.

"I keep hearing about this army Williams has. What about it, Quirt? Doesn't that seem a little weird to you?"

The man shrugged. "You ain't been in Texas long if you think that's weird. Hell, half the millionaires in this state have protection organizations that would do the Marines *and* the CIA proud. Most of them are just tough old boys who got lucky in the oil fields, Hawk. They may act rich, but they still think poor. Most of them got the idea everyone's out to rob what they got." The man grinned and stretched, yawning. "I guess it's true ol' Skate's gone a little overboard—they say he's got guns up to the house that can shoot down planes. Big planes. Maybe he just figures he had to work his ass off to get what he got, and now he's being damn careful he hangs on to it. That's why they call him 'Skate,' you know. Boys say they call him that 'cause when he was a young Tom, he had to skate through a ton of shit to pull himself out of the country slums."

"Yeah? What's his real first name?"

Quirt shrugged. "You'll have to ask someone who knows him better than me."

Trying not to act too interested, Hawker shrugged. "Well, I don't care what the man does—as long as he pays me my wages on time."

As Hawker turned to go Evans called after him, "Hey, Hawk?"

"Yeah?"

"If you're after a cold beer, you'll find the boys in Pearsall. If you're after something else, drive right on into San Antone. There's a house there called Flora and Ella's. Price up front will seem steep, but it'll save you money on penicillin later."

Hawker laughed in spite of his suspicions. "Thanks for the advice, Quirt. Flora and Ella's. I'll remember."

The moment Hawker started his pickup truck, Quirt Evans tossed down the magazine he was reading, strapped on his gun belt) then went outside to saddle his horse. . . .

TEN

In the mess hall of Ranch #4 there was a glossy wooden map showing all of Skate Williams's holdings.

Hawker had memorized the map and then resketched it in private.

As he bounced down the rutted south Texas road, he switched on the dome light and studied his sketch. The five secondary ranches were like spokes on a wheel, all orbiting around Ranch #1, Skate Williams's home.

It made it very hard to sneak down the long road that led only to Ranch #1—and no doubt it was planned that way.

Hawker wrestled with the problem as he drove. Finally he hit upon a likely solution. He slowed at the turnoff, then drove on past. He had hoped to find an abandoned barn in which to hide his truck, but there was none. He finally had to settle for a thick stand of sycamores by the shallow river, which flowed down out of the hills.

He got out of the truck. It was a still Texas night with blazing stars and a full moon.

Hawker could smell the fresh musk of the river as it *burpled* over stones.

Hawker jumped into the open bed of the truck. In the back of the truck he had had a Houston mechanic weld an oversize tool chest to the wall of the cab. The steel lid was padlocked shut, and now Hawker opened the lock.

Inside was the weaponry Jake Hayes had sent from Chicago. The one thing Hawker wasn't able to hide in the tool chest was his computer.

He wished he had it now—he would have run a check on Quirt Evans.

Hawker took what he thought he might need from the chest: an automatic weapon (with plenty of ammunition this time); a little Walther PPK automatic; a new Colt Commando automatic rifle in place of his customized Colt Commander, which he had lost in Mexico; his Randall knife; several spider-size listening transmitters; a rope with a grappling hook; wire cutters; three different varieties of state-of-the-art explosives; and several grenades.

He couldn't be sure that he would need any of it. In fact, he hoped he wouldn't. But, if he did need it he wanted it ready.

He packed the equipment carefully in a canvas knapsack, then sealed the chest again with the padlock.

Finally he opened the truck's hood and loosened a wire on the distributor cap. When he was sure the truck would not start, he left the hood open and headed off down the dirt road to Skate Williams's ranch.

For the first mile he stuck to the middle of the road. After all, he had a reasonable explanation for being where he was: His truck wouldn't start. But then, far ahead, he saw the sharp blue haze of mercury lights over what had to be a security gate.

Now he could no longer play the role of the one-armed man seeking help for his broken-down truck. Not if he was to find out what he needed to know.

Hawker tossed his cowboy hat into the ditch and stripped off the serape. He removed the chest guard and freed his right arm. Having his arm strapped to his chest all day was sheer misery, and it felt good to be able to move it again.

Hawker rolled the props of his disguise into the serape and hid it all in a clump of mesquite. To mark the area so he could find it quickly, he took out his Randall knife and cut two thin slashes on the backside of the fence post nearest the cache.

Finally he pulled on a black wool watch cap to keep the moon from reflecting off his red-brown hair, then he climbed the fence and set off across the pasture toward the Williams mansion.

It was his hope to be able to get an idea of just how well equipped and organized Skate Williams's so-called "army" really was. Also, he wanted to try to spot the slave houses and, if the opportunity presented itself, to make contact with one of the slaves and find out where they were keeping Cristoba de Abella.

But, more than anything else, he didn't want to get caught.

To get caught meant death. But, worse, it meant failure.

Hawker moved toward the security gate, parallel to the road and the fence.

Steers in the pasture were dark silhouettes that moved past him with a ghostly grace. The air smelled of fresh manure and the peppery odor of mesquite.

The pasture fence ended abruptly at a higher adobe fence

that began at the security gate and apparently encircled the whole estate. Hawker was on his belly now, hidden in the shadows of the higher fence.

From his position he could see that two guards sat within a lighted cubicle from within which the high wrought-iron gate was controlled. It was an extraordinary security precaution for such a secluded ranch.

Hawker wondered if Williams was just paranoid—or whether he had a reason to be expecting trouble.

The guards were dressed like soldiers, in plain green fatigues. They sat playing cards in the lighted guardhouse, and Hawker could see them plainly from his position outside. When one of them stood to get coffee, Hawker could see that he wore a side arm.

Both were Anglos, and both looked rugged and businesslike.

Hawker hoped they weren't indicative of all of Williams's troops. If they were, this mission would be even tougher than he had thought. Maybe even impossible.

On the wall behind the guards was a board covered with lights and toggle switches—no doubt a center for electronic surveillance. Hawker exhaled a long, low breath.

"Damn," he whispered to himself.

Getting in would be tough—and getting out tougher yet.

Hawker watched for a few minutes before taking out a sausage roll of plastic explosives and planting a heavy load behind a bush on the wall of the guardhouse.

That done, he turned to crawl along the outside of the high adobe fence. As he did, a high-powered searchlight was suddenly switched on, and the door of the guardhouse was thrown open as one of the guards ran out.

Immediately Hawker freed the brutal-looking Colt Commando rifle he carried on his back, and lifted it toward the first guard. The metal stock was cool against his cheek.

Through the soft red glow of the Colt's Star-Tron Night Vision System, Hawker watched the guard draw a military-type .45-caliber automatic.

Hawker waited for the searchlight to vector toward him. But it never did. Instead it was fixed on the main dirt road.

He listened, his own breath coming swift and shallow. Then he heard what the electronic listening system must have heard long before: the steady *clippity-clop* of a horse walking. Moments later, the horse and rider appeared in the harsh white light.

The rider, a tall, rangy man wearing a cowboy hat, held up his hand in greeting.

He said a few words to the guard, and there was the sound of laughter.

Then the huge wrought-iron gate swung open on an electric hinge, and the rider disappeared behind the adobe wall.

The gate was swung shut immediately.

Hawker waited a few minutes more, then crawled off into the darkness, his mind working at a frantic pace.

The man on the horse had been Quirt Evans. . . .

There was a chance that Evans *was* an informer—and that he had found Hawker's truck and now he was going to warn Williams.

But there was something in Quirt's easy manner as he greeted the guards that told Hawker that, informer or not, he hadn't come with any warnings.

One thing was for sure, though: Quirt was far too familiar with the guards for Hawker to believe he had met with Williams only twice.

Evans had lied. Also, he seemed to know a hell of a lot more about Hawker than he would come right out and say. But, if he did know why Hawker was at the Sister Star Ranch, why had he helped get him a job there? Why hadn't he spoken up immediately or—more reasonably—let Jeb kill him when he had had the chance?

None of it seemed to make any sense.

The only way to find out, Hawker was sure, was to slip into the inner sanctum of this slaver, tyrant, and survivalist supreme: Skate Williams.

The first problem was how to get over the wall. The adobe fence was undoubtedly keyed to some kind of electronic warning system. Hawker was sure that the moment he touched the top surface of the wall, alarms all over the estate would be sounded.

Once away from the guard outpost, he moved more quickly. The wind had freshened from the northwest, casting a thin cirrus scud toward the moon. The cattle seemed to grow more restless. There was the smell of coming rain in the wind.

At the back corner of the wall—about a quarter of a mile from the guard outpost—Hawker found what he was looking for. A giant oak grew within the Williams estate, but one high branch extended over the wall.

Hawker took the rope and grappling hook from his belt. It took him three throws to finally get the hook to wrap around the limb.

Motionless, he waited to make sure no one had heard him.

It was ten-fifteen by the green glow of his Seiko diver's watch.

After a full two minutes he pulled himself up the rope, hand over hand. The limb was about twenty feet off the ground. It seemed higher.

When he got to the limb, he swung his legs over, straddling it. Then he pulled the rope up behind him, buckled it into his belt, and worked his way to the trunk of the tree.

From that height he could see the bright windows of the main house. It was three stories high with massive pillars.

According to the talk around the bunkhouse, Williams was a widower with no children. Hawker wondered why he had such a large house and, moreover, why there were so many lights on.

Did Williams's troops live with him? That didn't seem likely. And, if they did, what were those long, bunk-house-style houses lighted behind the main house? There must have been a half-dozen of them.

Before Hawker climbed down the tree, he took a long look through the Star-Tron Night Vision System, which was mounted as a scope on the Colt Commando rifle. The Star-Tron, manufactured by Smith & Wesson, collected all available night light—moon and star glow, house lights, etc.—and magnified it a total of eighty-five thousand times via an intensifier tube. The final image, as sharply contrasted as high noon but an eerie red, was formed on an interior screen but viewed through an eyepiece like an ordinary rifle scope.

Hawker was glad he'd taken the precaution of looking through the Star-Tron.

Along with the guards at the gate, Skate Williams had posted foot guards to walk the perimeter of the interior wall. The guards patrolled alone, but in an overlapping system that meant they were due to pass each other every so many minutes—a built-in system of checks.

To jump one guard was to alert all the guards.

Two guards, coming from opposite directions, approached the large oak tree now.

Slowly Hawker lowered the Commando rifle. Because they walked in the shadow of the adobe wall, they were invisible to the naked eye. Hawker patted the Star-Tron in genuine appreciation.

When the guards were about fifteen yards away, Hawker heard the crack of twigs and the creak of leather, and then they came into view beneath the tree in which he sat.

"Merriwald?"

"Yeah. Hawser?"

"You got it."

The two men stopped beneath the tree. Looking down on them, Hawker got only the impression of two sets of narrow shoulders and fatigue hats.

"Hey, I've got to stop and have a smoke."

"Come on, you know the rules about that, Hawser."

"And you're going to squeal, right, Merriwald?" The man snorted in disgust and put away the pack of cigarettes. "Boy, I'm telling you, you people really are a pain in the ass."

"You knew the rules before you joined, Hawser. If you don't like it, tell Mr. Williams—"

"No thanks, man. I *know* how he discharges guys." Hawser seemed suddenly nervous. "Hey, look, Merriwald, you're not gonna report me for this, are you? Hell, all I was going to do was have a little smoke."

Merriwald grew more prim as he realized he now had Hawser in his power. "We've got important work to do, Hawser. Work that's more important than you, me, or any one person. Even a little thing, like smoking on patrol, could jeopardize it all. Especially on a night like tonight, with a big shipment going out from the farm."

"Yeah?" Hawser sounded impressed. "Hell, I didn't even know there was a shipment going out. Shit, if I'd known—"

"And you might watch your language while you're at it," Merriwald snapped. "You haven't been here long, but you should have realized by now that we try to keep things nice and clean. That's the way it *should* be, Hawser, and I, for one, don't like the way you talk. And this is the only warning I'm going to give you—"

"Hey, Merriwald," Hawser cut in, trying to change the subject. "Why all the fuss about a shipment? Shipments go out of here all the time."

"This isn't a beef shipment, that's why. This is straight stuff. It's going right to the streets—but that's none of my concern, and it's certainly none of your concern." Hawker watched Merriwald check his watch. "We're both exactly a minute and forty seconds behind schedule because of you, Hawser. Now snap to, or we'll miss our next rendezvous."

"Okay, Merriwald, as long as I got your word you're not going to report me. . . ."

Merriwald marched off before the other man had a chance to finish. When Merriwald was out of earshot, Hawser added in a whisper, "You donkey dick." Then he walked away in the opposite direction.

Hawker followed their progress through the Star-Tron. When they were well away, he climbed down from the tree. Carrying the Colt Commando automatic ready at hip level, he headed for the main house.

He had hoped to get in and out without leaving the slightest clue that he had been there. But now, with all the security and all the guards, he had to admit there wasn't much chance of that.

And he was right.

Trouble was all too soon in coming. . . .

ELEVEN

The guard captured him as he neared the main house. Hawker was doubly surprised because he had just checked the area ahead through the Star-Tron.

The guard must have been staked out behind the massive garage.

As Hawker edged along the side of the garage, a cold voice stopped him? *"Freeze.* Put down your weapon, then place your hands against the wall. *Now."*

The voice came from about ten feet behind him. Hawker hesitated, then realized he had no choice. To try to shoot it out would have brought a dozen other guards on the run.

Slowly Hawker placed the Colt Commando on the ground, then leaned his hands against the side of the garage.

"The side arm, too, buddy. And that knapsack you're carrying."

There was a nervous quiver in the guard's voice. Hawker found that reassuring. He lifted the Walther out of its little holster and dropped it in the dirt beside his pack.

Gravel crunched beneath the guard's feet as he came closer.

He kicked Hawker's feet wider apart, then began to frisk him with his left hand.

Hawker knew it was now or never.

He waited until the guard ran his hand beneath his left armpit. When he did, Hawker locked down with his left arm and spun with all his weight. The guard was slammed into the wall, and Hawker immediately grabbed his right wrist and twisted the pistol away.

In that microsecond Hawker saw the guard's mouth open wide to scream a warning.

But the warning was never voiced. Hawker slammed his right fist into the man's face, then jumped on top of him when he hit the ground.

They wrestled violently in the sand, and then Hawker realized the guard now had a knife. It seemed to appear in his hand as if by magic. Hawker ducked away as it speared past his face, then he locked both hands on the guard's right arm.

It was a five-second test of strength, which seemed to last forever. And, in fact, it did—for the guard.

The vigilante forced the blade of the knife downward, downward, downward. When the guard realized he was going to lose, his whole body gave a desperate jolt, trying to roll away from beneath Hawker.

But too late.

With an effort that made his muscles creak, Hawker forced the blade of the knife deep into the guard's throat. The guard thrashed wildly in the sand as Hawker rolled away.

There was a raspy, deflating hiss, like a balloon losing air. The guard's mouth worked, but no sound escaped.

Hawker realized his hands were wet and sticky: blood.

He wiped them on the guard's fatigue pants, then waited for a long minute to make sure their fight had not drawn the attention of the other guards.

It hadn't.

Now hurrying, Hawker pulled the guard's body into the garage, then picked up his gear and moved on toward the main house.

The house looked even bigger now. A mansion in the tradition of the Old South. A spotlight at the base of the flagpole in the grassy circle out front showed the Lone Star banner of Texas.

The flag snapped in the wind of the approaching storm.

A massive porch ran the breadth of the mansion, and Hawker crawled into the bushes beside it and poked his head over to have a look.

A guard sat in a chair outside the front door. His rifle leaned against the wall behind him. Once again Hawker was discouraged by the knowledge that getting to Skate Williams would be no easy task.

As he knelt there in the darkness, he heard the brass tumble of a lock, and then watched as the front door was pulled open.

The guard jumped quickly to his feet at full attention.

"Good evening, Mr. Williams!" the guard greeted formally.

A gigantic man stepped onto the porch. Hawker could see him plainly in the light from the front window. He wore a gray Stetson hat and a dark western-cut suit. Dwarfed in his right hand was the glowing eye of a long Presidente cigar. The man had a hog-size face, all eyes and jowls, which wore a pinched, surly expression. His nose, positioned oddly close to his eyes, was potato-shaped and, at some time in the past, had been knocked off center. The sideburns that bristled from beneath the Stetson were sandy-colored, professionally styled.

Hawker guessed Skate Williams to be in his early sixties.

"At ease, sergeant." The man put the cigar in his mouth and patted his mountainous stomach as if he had just finished a good meal. "Did Roy Dalton show up?"

"Been here all evening, sir. He's over at Ranch Number Three."

"What about Quirt Evans?"

"Rode in about thirty minutes ago."

"Good. And the trucks?"

"Over with Dalton, waiting to be loaded on your orders, sir."

The wooden deck of the porch creaked beneath the man's weight as he walked toward the steps. "Get on the horn and tell them I'll be a little late." There was an obscene edge to his snicker. "The doctor tells me our little *señorita* is just about healed."

The guard allowed himself a smile. "Yes, sir. Very good, sir. I'll tell them you're still at dinner and will be there in . . . about an hour?"

The big man grinned. "Good man, sergeant. Yeah, an hour ought to just about do it." His laugh was phlegmy. "The doctor says this girl is still a virgin."

Hawker ducked into the bushes as Skate Williams rumbled past. He could feel the anger move through him in a surge of adrenaline. He felt the strong urge to step out in front of the man and cut him in two with the Colt Commando.

There could be only one *"señorita"* on the ranch who fit the implied description.

Cristoba de Abella.

Because of the bullet wound, she had been put under a doctor's care, and now she was sufficiently healed for Skate Williams to use as his toy.

Hawker forced his anger under control as he watched the big man waddle past.

There was no place for anger on a mission such as this. There were too many unknown factors to go rushing in, guns blazing.

No, taking Skate Williams apart called for patience and professionalism instead of anger.

For now, anyway.

Keeping a safe distance, Hawker tailed the giant Texan.

He had waited by the porch only long enough to plant a two-fisted chunk of plastic explosives under the foundation of the house. After inserting the detonator, he had crept off after Williams.

Williams followed a brick path around the garage. There was a moment of suspense as he hesitated and seemed to realize that a guard was no longer posted there.

But then he moved on, the smell of his big cigar overpowering the smell of rain in the wind.

A hundred yards behind the main house were a half-dozen long bunkhouse-type buildings. As they drew closer, Hawker could see that Williams housed at least part of his security force there.

Guards stood at attention in the parade yard in front of each barracks. For an uncomfortable moment, Hawker thought Williams was going to lead him right through the parade ground.

But he turned abruptly through a high maze of shrubs, and once again Hawker felt the urge to jump the man here; to fight him hand-to-hand and kill him. There was reason enough: Williams bought, sold, and enslaved human beings; he lived by no laws save his own; he acquired land and mineral rights through force and intimidation, preying on people as innocent as Sancho Rigera—people who wanted nothing more than to live and raise their families.

And once again Hawker fought off the urge.

There was still too much he needed to know. What was this "shipment" he had heard about? And why were there trucks waiting at this mysterious Ranch #3, Williams's experimental farm?

Staying a safe thirty yards away, Hawker crept along behind.

Hidden away in a secluded copse was a small white cottage. A porch light was on, and Hawker noted that there were bars on the windows. A guard stood outside. As Williams approached, the guard snapped to attention.

"Is the girl awake?" Skate Williams asked, not even bothering to return the salute.

"I wouldn't know, sir. She's been very quiet."

"How long ago did the doctor leave?"

"Two hours, maybe."

Williams nodded. "Look, private, I want you to report to Ranch Number Three."

"But, sir, my superior told me that under no circumstances was I to leave this post—"

Williams grabbed the man by the collar so quickly that it surprised even Hawker. He shook the smaller soldier the way a terrier might shake a rat. *"I'm* your superior, you dumb little shit. And you'll do exactly as I say!"

"Yes, sir!" the guard shouted mechanically. "Right away, sir!"

Williams released him and then turned to watch as the guard hustled off toward the brick path. As he hurried away, Williams dropped his cigar on the floor of the porch and ground it out with the heel of his boot. With a glance over his shoulder he took out a ring of keys, unlocked the door, and went inside.

Hawker wanted to follow. But he couldn't. Not right away, because the guard was coming straight at him.

The vigilante forced his way into the bushes. His left foot caught on a root and he fell backward. The Colt Commando snagged itself in the thicket and hung by its sling above him.

"Who goes there?" the guard challenged in a half-whisper.

Hawker slowly reached for the assault rifle overhead. The noise the branches made when he moved seemed deafening, and he stopped.

"Hey? Who's in there?"

In front of him the beam of a flashlight swept the bushes, and then there was a rifle barrel stabbing at him, a foot from his face. The guard knelt, peering into the thicket, and his eyes grew wide when he saw Hawker.

"Who in the hell—"

The guard never got a chance to finish his question. Hawker grabbed the rifle barrel and jerked the man into the bushes on top of him. He wrestled the weapon free, but he could not unseat the guard.

The guard hit him twice in the face, hard. As Hawker

brought his hands up to block the next flurry of punches, the guard locked his hands around Hawker's throat.

Standing next to the bulk of Skate Williams, the guard hadn't impressed Hawker as being particularly big.

But he had a grip like a bear trap.

Catching his wrists cross-handed, Hawker punched the man's hands away from his neck, then slid his thumbs inside the man's cheeks and ripped with all his strength.

The man's scream was more like a hiss of anguish, and Hawker was thankful for that. Having his cheeks pulled open had taken the fight out of him, and now the guard wanted only to get away. As he turned to crawl safely out of the bushes, Hawker grabbed him by the back of the shirt and jerked him back. He drew the little Walther and used the butt to club him twice behind the ear.

The guard kicked once, then lay still.

Hawker pushed the dead weight of the man off him, recovered the assault rifle, then checked to see if the man's body could be seen from the brick path.

It couldn't.

Hawker hurried on toward the cottage, keeping low.

The front door was closed once again, and the light inside was brighter. Hawker knelt at the porch, then crawled around to the back window and looked through the bars inside.

What he saw both gladdened and sickened him.

Cristoba de Abella was there. Still alive. Healthy. In good shape except for the strip of gauze bandage on her left arm. She stood beside a narrow bed. There was a lamp on the desk, which threw a soft yellow light over the room. In that first moment Hawker realized that he had underestimated her beauty.

She wore a sheer white nightgown that came down to her thighs. Her legs were long and nut-colored, and in the light he could see that a soft, peach-hued fuzz grew on them. Her hair was blue-black, combed long to the small of her back, and it glistened in the light. Beneath the translucent nightgown, her breasts were abrupt swells, firm and heavy, that peaked at the dark expanse of nipple.

Her face seemed more striking than he remembered: the sculptured Indio nose and cheeks; the soft curve of chin; the proud Mayan eyes, like brown liquid pools, which were devoid of all human emotion.

Except for now.

Now the eyes of the young Cristoba de Abella showed more than fear. They showed loathing and disgust—and terror.

Skate Williams stood before her, dwarfing her. He had stripped off his jacket and shirt. His belly was covered with hair, a massive gray blob. His trousers were down around his ankles and, ludicrously, he wore European-style red bikini shorts.

His big hands were on Cristoba's shoulders, and Hawker could hear his voice through the window.

"Now look at it from my point of view, *señorita*, darling." Williams smiled. "When they brought you in here, you was damaged goods. Had that nasty little bullet hole through the meat of your arm. I could have let you die. Could have just told that greasy Mexican to cart you on back to that nice little bar down Rio Bravo way. They got a show there with a dog and a big nigger—and they'd'a had you on that stage the next day." His smile broadened. "But, instead, out of the goodness of my heart I took you in. Had a fine doctor tend you. And, hell, it was *you* who promised that if we didn't stick no needles in you to make you more . . . loyal . . . you'd be extra real nice to me." The smile vanished, and he shook her roughly. "Well, darlin', we didn't stick no needles in you, and now you'd damn well better be nice to me. Real nice. And I mean right now."

Cristoba gave a low, throaty moan of revulsion as Williams's hand slid down her arm and found her breast, squeezing it roughly.

She tried to pull away. "Don't," she pleaded. "Please. That hurts."

Williams leaned over her, kissing the young girl's neck. "Then be nice to me, Cristy, baby. Get down on your knees and be nice—"

"No!" The girl tried to jerk away, and as she did, her face turned toward the window where Hawker now stood. She saw him then, her eyes growing wide in recognition, and her one free arm reached out as if yearning to take Hawker's hand. But then Williams pulled her back and ripped the gown from her shoulders and clamped his wide mouth on her pale breast.

Hawker saw no more because he was running. Running toward the front door of the cottage. Running, not caring any longer for the mission or the unanswered questions. Running with but one thought: to get his hands on Skate Williams and to kill him; kill him slowly.

But as he slid around the corner of the cottage, the Colt assault rifle at hip level and ready, several things happened at once.

The searing beam of a searchlight caught him full in the face. Then a siren screamed a long, continuous wail from somewhere near the main house, like an old World War II warning to head for the bomb shelters.

The firecracker crackle of automatic weapons fire erupted from a line of trees several hundred yards away, kicking up tufts of dirt far in front of Hawker.

In that sudden chaos Hawker still had but one thought: to get inside, kill Williams, and free the girl.

But as he reached for the railing to swing himself up on the porch, Williams charged halfway out the door, his pants still down. In the microsecond it took him to realize Hawker was not one of his men, he fired two quick shots from the heavy-caliber revolver in his right hand.

Hawker ducked, then sprayed the door with a quick burst of the Commando. But too late. Williams had ducked back inside.

Hawker stood with the intention of shooting away the lock, but a flurry of slugs from more guards splintered the wood on the porch in front of him. He could see them running at him: a dozen guards, all with heavy weapons, all firing at once.

He could do nothing but retreat.

And run. Run for his life and take as many of the guards with him as he could.

As Hawker reluctantly trotted toward the darkness of the ranch's back acreage, he heard the high, pleading scream of the girl: "Help me! Oh, please, you must help me!"

I will, Hawker thought as he held the assault rifle on full automatic, and three more guards fell in his wake. *Hang on for just one more night, Cristoba, and I will. I promise. . . .*

TWELVE

The next two hours were a nightmare as James Hawker ran the gauntlet of his life.

It was like barging through a forest filled with hornets' nests. Every twenty yards, it seemed, he stumbled into a new one.

Twice he tried to work his way back to the cottage in which Cristoba was imprisoned. And twice a fresh charge of guards pushed him back.

Finally Hawker had to admit that he had no choice but to make a fighting retreat. He couldn't do anyone any good if he was captured or killed.

Hawker lost the first set of guards in the best way he knew how. Running toward the back acreage of Williams's inner estate, Hawker took cover behind a stone bench and rummaged in his knapsack until he found what he was looking for.

He was in, he realized absently, some kind of ornamental garden. He wondered if any of the men chasing him had ever guessed they might die in such a pretty spot.

In a few seconds the guards came fanning down the hill,

shoulder to shoulder. They fired only sporadic bursts now, a covering fire to clear the path ahead.

Hawker waited until they were about forty-five yards away, then pulled the pins from two M-34 incendiary/fragmentation grenades. The M-34 is one of the most deadly grenades ever manufactured by the Department of Defense. It kills two ways. The rolled steel body is serrated to help fragmentation. And the four hundred twenty-five grams of white phosphorous filler burns at twenty-seven hundred degrees Centigrade for approximately one minute.

If the shrapnel doesn't get you, the fire will.

The grenades work on a four-second delay system, so Hawker counted to a nervy "one-thousand-three" and then hurled them overhanded in quick succession.

There was an almost simultaneous double explosion followed by a blinding white light.

Hawker knew what was coming, so he turned away. Even so, his peripheral vision caught the shocking brightness of the light and saw the handful of men wither beneath its heat.

Caught within that fiery white hell, their screams were short-lived.

Hawker punched a fresh clip into the Colt Commando, adjusted the knapsack over his shoulder, and continued uninterrupted to the back adobe wall.

Hawker knew that by climbing the wall he might pinpoint his position for Williams's men. The electronic security system was certainly sophisticated enough. But he couldn't worry about that now. He unbelted the grappling hook, tossed it over the wall, then climbed hand over hand to the top.

What he saw on the other side surprised him. He expected to see Ranch #3, and he did. But what surprised him was that Ranch #3 looked nothing like the other ranches. Since it was supposed to be an experimental farm, he expected to see barns and outbuildings.

There were none of these things.

Instead he saw what looked like a single large factory complex surrounded by miles and miles of greenhouses. The greenhouses weren't the glass structures he had seen in the Chicago area. These were shielded by translucent nets, under which heat lights blazed beneath sprinkler systems. Through the nets Hawker could see long rows of what looked to be sapling trees.

What in the hell was Williams growing? he wondered. It wasn't marijuana. And it sure as hell wasn't poppies. But what else would explain the conversation he had heard between the two guards about a "shipment" leaving tonight?

For the moment Hawker didn't have time to give it much thought. As he dropped from the wall he heard a muffled voice call out, "There he is!"

Immediately shots exploded from the heavy mesquite brush that covered the field between Hawker and the distant greenhouses. Hawker jumped to his feet, ran a zigzag course, then dove into the cover of the wiry mesquite.

Sighting through the Star-Tron scope, Hawker surveyed the field before him.

Had the situation not been so dangerous, Hawker would have smiled at how Williams's soldiers stood out in the owlish vision of the Star-Tron.

He could see all six of them very plainly. They knelt or lay in what they thought to be the protective shadows of the mesquite. In the eerie red glow of the Star-Tron Hawker watched what he assumed was the team leader signal for two of his men to move forward.

As they moved Hawker prepared to change positions quickly before calling out to the men, "Hey! Freeze right where you are and listen, because I'm only going to say this once. I'm going to give you assholes one chance to drop your weapons and let me pass, because if you don't—"

They never allowed him to finish. Heavy weapons fire ripped wildly through the cover, seeking his voice.

Hawker dived, rolled, and dived again before coming up on one knee, the assault rifle at ready.

He had given them their chance to get the hell out alive. And they had refused.

Hawker brought the 135mm Star-Tron to bear on the chest of the leader. Because the Colt Commando is a shortened version of the M-16, its accuracy is not quite as good. It was built for tough in-fighting and tight situations. But Williams's soldiers were only about fifty yards away, so Hawker didn't require pinpoint accuracy. He brought the cross hairs to bear on the team leader's chest, squeezed off two careful shots, and the team leader dropped as if he had been magically deboned.

Hawker waited to see if the others had figured out what was going to happen to them.

The heavy return of fire told him they hadn't. . . .

Shooting sitting ducks wasn't Hawker's idea of sport. But this wasn't sport. It was war.

One by one, Hawker brought the Star-Tron scope vectoring on each man in the squad, and the 5.56mm slugs smacked through their flesh traveling at eight hundred eighty meters per second, more than twice the speed of sound.

When the dirty work was done, Hawker got to his feet and jogged through the thick mesquite toward the factorylike building in the distance.

From every direction, it seemed, came the haunting wail of sirens. A thin smile touched Hawker's sweat-streaked face. Skate Williams had had his big dinner, and he had planned on a night of fun with the pretty little Indio girl from south of the border. A night of recreation spiced with the perverted allure of rape.

Well, Hawker was going to give him a night of recreation. But the only thing going to be raped was Williams's confused little army.

From the woods, now behind him, Hawker could hear the alto hacking of dogs. He knew that the men at Ranch #3 would be on full alert: Stop unknown attacker or attackers from exiting the compound. Those would be the logical orders. But those orders, in reality, were to his advantage.

Hawker thought about it as he ran. The security force from the main ranch would be coming after him in a wave through the woods. But the soldiers from Ranch #3 would probably be spread out around the fence that no doubt enclosed the area. If he could draw all their fire toward the center of the compound, he might be able to find a way to slip out unseen while they traded shots with each other. . . .

It sounded good.

But, as always, he would have to play it by ear.

As Hawker ran he realized, oddly, how much more . . . *alive*

. . . he felt in these situations of life and death. His concentration was total. His objective was always perfectly clear. There were no half-truths; no dingy grays of reality. There was only the clarity of his mission: to succeed completely or fail totally. And everything depended on his physical strength, his endurance, and his intellect.

There were no time-outs in this game. No rules; no disputed calls; no second chances.

In such a conflict every moment seemed distilled. Every minute seemed pure. He enjoyed perfect communication between body and mind.

Sometimes Hawker told himself he had become a vigilante because there were great wrongs in the country that needed to be righted. Even to himself he sometimes played the role of the middle-American knight in slightly tarnished armor, the beer-drinking patron of the week, the terrorized, and the leaderless. And while it was true that there were great wrongs being committed, and some of them could only be righted by a vigilante, Hawker couldn't pretend those were the only reasons.

It was in the rare moments that he understood it best; the singular moments of honesty and clarity, such as this one, when he admitted to himself why he really did what he did. He did it because it was what he did best.

And he loved it.

Ahead was the first line of greenhouses. Hawker slowed by the first one and looked in. The covering was made of a common black screen that reduced the harshness of the sun. Inside were about a dozen rows of thin trees, twenty to a row. The trees were about twelve to fifteen feet tall with shiny, thick stems and short, pale green leaves. Spaced above every row of trees were bare light bulbs and a sprinkler system made of PVC pipe. The trees were planted in black plastic buckets and there were plastic tubes looping into each bucket: a hydroponic feeding system.

A nursery?

For a moment Hawker couldn't believe it. This is what the mysterious Ranch #3 was—a nursery? He rubbed his chin. It didn't make any sense. Why the heavy security? Certainly there had to be more at stake than the weird story he had heard of Skate Williams's preparation for the coming world collapse.

But what?

Hawker stripped a couple of leaves off one tree and held them to his nose. They smelled good—like fresh tea leaves. He bit a small piece of one leaf, chewed it, then spat. The leaf was bitter, and it immediately numbed his tongue.

There was, something here that touched one of Hawker's memory electrodes. Some past bit of information; some subject he had once done a good bit of reading on.

And suddenly he remembered.

Suddenly he realized what it was all about.

It finally made sense: the slave laborers, the factory, the army, the ingenious franchise system—everything. When illuminated by the knowledge of Skate Williams's greed, everything fell neatly into place.

Hawker's one problem was that he had underestimated the man's greed. And his ruthlessness. And his cleverness.

But now it all made sense.

Williams *did* have it all: oil, water, produce, and beef. Especially beef—if Hawker was right. But what else explained the conversation he had heard between the two guards? Something about tonight's shipment going straight to the streets? What else answered the implied question: Where did it go when it *didn't* go straight to the streets?

Williams had indeed developed a practical method to take control of a massive cross section of the American public.

As nauseating as his method was, Williams had found the final solution to the question of total control.

And that was his goal, as Hawker now knew—total control. Skate Williams didn't just want to be a big man in Texas; he wanted to be the biggest man in the country.

And he had discovered a way to insure he would be just that.

Unless Hawker found a way to stop him.

Hawker stepped from beneath the screen, his resolve newly fired. If Skate Williams was doing what he suspected, he *had* to be stopped. Stopped now before it was too late—if it wasn't too late already.

Hawker surveyed the area. How many greenhouses were there? The acreage beyond the factory was filled with row after row of them. In the Texas night they glowed like a small city.

Thousands of them. Hundreds of thousands of trees. All growing right here in the land of good ol' boys and middle-class morality.

Who would have ever suspected?

Which is probably why Williams thought of it.

Hawker quickly took a couple more leaves and shoved them in his pocket, then hurried on toward the factory.

The sound of the dogs was getting closer. Ahead of him, where he hoped the fence would be, Hawker could see flashlight beams waving through a high dark cloud of oaks. Far off to his right he could hear the mechanical thump of a helicopter starting up.

Williams wasn't holding anything back. He wanted the intruder and he wanted him badly. Hawker wouldn't have been the least bit surprised to see a tank come busting through the trees, turret swinging.

It meant he had to get out, and get out just as quickly as he could. Because the sooner he got out, the sooner he could return, free Cristoba, and, with help, destroy what in time would no doubt become a symbol of hell to a nation of unsuspecting people.

Hawker hurried on.

The factory was the size of two barns, built of corrugated steel. The smoke that drifted out of the stacks blurred the pale moon. The smoke had an odd smell. Like burned toast.

A high chain-link fence topped with barbed wire surrounded the factory.

Hawker found the wire cutters in the knapsack and snipped the barbed wire away so he could climb over.

He wondered if there were any guards left on station to hear the alarms go off.

There were.

And finding out almost cost Hawker his life. . . .

THIRTEEN

He had hoped to break into the factory and confirm his suspicions that the building was really more than just a processing plant.

But he never got the chance.

As he reached to turn the knob the main door flew open. Hawker's foot caught most of the impact, but the metal door still cracked him in the face hard enough to send him stumbling sideways. As he did, a heavy-caliber revolver poked out through the opening and exploded right by his cheek.

Hawker's ears rang; his head buzzed—but he still managed to grab the guard's arm and twist as he fell, snapping the gun from his hand.

The guard was immediately on top of him, flailing away with his fists. Hawker pulled the guard tight against him, so the man's punches couldn't build much momentum.

"You're a dead man, you son of a bitch," the guard hissed as he smacked Hawker a glancing blow on the forehead. "I guarantee it: You're a fucking corpse."

Hawker grabbed the man by the shirt, shoved as if to push him away, then used the man's own resistance to roll him over his head. Hawker back-somersaulted with him so that their positions were immediately reversed.

As he rolled he drew the Walther automatic in one smooth motion. When the guard's lips opened in an involuntary expression of fear, Hawker shoved the short barrel into his mouth. "Your guarantees aren't worth much, friend," Hawker said. His voice was cold, unemotional.

The man gurgled an unintelligible reply.

"Was that some kind of apology, sport?"

The man's eyes were wide with terror. He shook his head up and down quickly and gurgled some more.

"Fine," said Hawker. "I think we're finally starting to communicate." He pulled the Walther from the guard's mouth. "I'm going to tell you exactly what I want from you. Ready?"

"Sure," the guard said. "Anything. Hey, look, I wasn't really going to bump you off. I was just trying to scare you a little before I took you in—"

"Knock off the bullshit," Hawker snapped. "I've spent the evening getting to know how Williams's mercenaries try to scare people. Now get to your feet and make it quick. Your buddies are going to be showing up soon, and at my parties, the first to arrive is usually the first to check out. And you were the first to arrive, friend."

The guard held his hands over his head even though Hawker had not yet ordered him to do so. It was a submissive gesture. Hawker stood eye to eye with him: a big man with abrupt, unattractive features and a lot of wiry black hair. "Anything, pal. Anything you want. Just don't shoot me, for God's sake."

Hawker motioned toward the factory door. "I want a quick tour of the plant. A meat-processing plant, isn't it?"

"What? No. No, the meat-processing plant is over on the—" The guard caught himself, eyes narrowing. "Hey, how did you know about that? Who in the hell are you, anyway?"

Hawker grabbed him by the shoulder and swung him around. He pushed him roughly toward the door. "Let's just pretend I'm your friendly representative from the USDA. Now get moving."

Hawker opened the door, and the two of them stepped inside. The plant was an open, functional building, dimly lit. In the weak light he could see conveyor belts and what appeared to be a series of metal trays the size of small cars. The trays sat over banks of propane burners. These would be used for drying the leaves.

"You keep the red gas in another building?" Hawker demanded.

The guard didn't answer immediately. He seemed to be looking for something—or someone. Noticing it, Hawker holstered the Walther, and lifted the Colt Commando from his shoulder.

"I asked you a question. The red gas. Where do you keep it?"

"If you know so much, why do you have to ask?"

The guard was stalling.

Hawker touched the automatic rifle to the back of the man's head. "One more smart answer, friend, and you're going to spend the rest of eternity saying grace through your asshole."

"The red gas," the guard said slowly, his attention obviously someplace else. "We use it in the processing. First you have to toast the leaves, and then you—"

That's when Hawker saw it coming. A lean black shape

charging noiselessly through the shadows. Then he could hear the whisper of its paws on the cement floor as it sprinted toward him, and then he could see the Doberman's teeth bared as it gaited into the pale circle of light.

"*Vampire—kill!*" commanded the guard as he tried to twist away from Hawker.

As the dog's feet left the ground Hawker caught the guard's shirt collar and pulled him into the animal's path, like a shield. The Doberman was already in mid-flight, its jaws locked wide. It hit the guard neck-high, and for a frightening moment, Hawker thought the hot squirt of blood he felt was his own.

It wasn't.

The guard gave a gurgling scream as he fell to the ground, the dog still on him, teeth gnashing, wild and confused with blood frenzy. The slash in the man's throat spurted black liquid with ever-weakening velocity as his heart emptied.

Hawker raised his rifle, ready to kill the dog, but then a sputtering flash of fire and the hammer-smack of slugs piercing the wall behind him sent Hawker backing out the door.

A guard on the second level of the plant had opened fire on him. There was the echo of men running on metal, and Hawker knew the guard was not alone.

He squeezed off a short burst in the direction of the fire. There was a guttural scream, a short vacancy of sound, and then the sickening thud of flesh hitting cement.

Hawker let the door slam shut behind him.

He had to move, and move quickly now, and he had to keep an eye on the front door of the factory. Every time it opened, Hawker pinned it shut with a short burst of fire.

From his knapsack, he took out a red sausage roll of plastic explosives. As he ran he kept his eye open for likely-looking spots. He found five of them, all well shielded and out of the eye of any casual observer.

He planted heavy chunks of the explosive, inserting electronic detonators into each. He put the largest charge behind a water-tank-size cylinder of what he assumed was red gas. Stenciled all around the tank were warnings:

DANGER

NO SMOKING

EXTREMELY FLAMMABLE

The explosives would give Skate Williams and his boys the surprise of their lives. And deaths.

But not tonight.

Tomorrow night. Tomorrow night when he returned freshly armed to get Cristoba.

It would be easier then. Easier in the chaos and confusion of the day after; a day when they would be expecting anything but a second assault.

Behind him now, Hawker could see the wave of men coming toward him. Maybe twenty of them. The dogs were out front, casting like pointers on their long leashes.

Hawker intentionally stepped beneath the red haze of the yard light. He lofted a few rounds of harmless fire at them, drawing their attention.

When they saw him, they returned the fire, charging at him. He saw one of them talk into a radio.

He would be notifying the guards on the front fence of Ranch #3 that they had spotted the intruder. He would be telling them to draw in from the other side.

Good. That's just what he wanted them to do.

Hawker dug out an M-18 colored-smoke grenade from his knapsack. He fired as he ran, making sure they would see him sprint toward the front door of the factory. Just before he got to the door, he pulled the pin on the M-18 and rolled it behind him.

The grenade sputtered, flared, and a thick shield of bright green smoke billowed out.

The screen would only last a minute and a half. And that didn't give him much time. Hawker knew the guards would figure he had done either of two things: taken cover inside the factory or followed the green smoke to the side fence.

He did neither.

He sprinted around to the back of the building and cut the barbed wire. As he climbed over he could hear automatic rifle fire, and then the return of fire.

The guards from inside the plant would be trading fire with those outside the plant. There was no way they could know he was only one man. For all the guards in the factory knew, they were being attacked by a horde of federal agents—or Russians, for that matter.

Hawker dropped down off the fence and moved off through the shadows. About half a mile from the factory, Hawker skirted long rows of cheaply built housing. They were like long, low dormitories, painted white. The dormitories were enclosed by chain-link fence and high strands of barbed wire. Hawker guessed there was enough cramped housing for maybe two hundred people.

A mass of Hispanics stood outside the dormitories, their noses pressed against the fencing. They were the slaves. Their clothing was shabby, and they all reminded Hawker just a little of animals he had seen in the zoo. Animals that had once roamed wild with the power of freedom but now, entrapped, had shrunken within themselves as they lived on nothing but memories.

For a moment Hawker considered freeing them. A kind of diversion. The guards wouldn't know who to go after, Hawker or the running slaves.

But it was not a good idea. Not on this night. The guards would shoot wildly at anyone not wearing a uniform. Hawker could free them, but he would free many of them only to run to their deaths.

Their escape would have to wait. Wait for a bigger diversion.

And Hawker knew just what the diversion would be.

He studied the layout of the slave prison once more, then trotted around to the back portion of the fence. The Hispanics followed him inside the fence.

"Do any of you speak English?" he yelled.

"I do. I speak good English." A thin young man, probably in his early twenties, pushed his way to the front of the crowd.

Hawker was rummaging through his knapsack. He brought out a small chunk of the plastic explosives. He said, "Sometime this week you're going to see a bright red flare. It could be day or night. The moment you see that flare, make sure everyone is away from this section of fence because I'm going to blow it open shortly afterward." Hawker molded the plastic explosives around the section of fence. "You got that?"

The young man nodded. "You're going to free us?"

"Yeah. Now listen! I want you to run directly toward the back adobe wall. There will be another hole there. Run through it and just keep on running. I'll try to have transportation waiting for you, but there are no guarantees. But whatever you do, don't try to stay and fight. No matter what happens. Just run. Okay?"

The young man was translating as Hawker spoke. He saw fresh light come to the eyes of those who listened, and for a moment he felt badly about not giving them more specific information. But he couldn't take the chance. Williams might have another plant hidden among them.

"We will do what you say, amigo!" the young man called after him. He added something else, but Hawker didn't hear.

He was already running.

The same kind of high adobe wall enclosed Ranch #3. With the guards occupied at the factory, Hawker had no trouble planting a larger charge of explosives before climbing over.

After that, he struck off through the pasture. The steers provided cover—if he needed cover. He was just one more dark shape moving in the moonlight.

At intervals, he checked the terrain ahead through the Star-Tron scope to make sure no surprises awaited him.

Hawker was getting awfully tired of surprises.

As he headed back toward his truck, he toyed with the idea of resuming his identity as the one-armed drifter. After all, Williams's men would be looking for a man with two arms. Two good arms.

For a moment Hawker thought that seeing the reactions of Roy Dalton and Quirt Evans might actually be worth the risk.

But then he decided that would be cutting it too close. After all, Evans was already suspicious of him. And he seemed to know more than he would come out and say.

No, he would make his break tonight. Maybe get in his truck, drive to the nearest town and call Sancho Rigera—if they hadn't found his truck.

Yes, that would be the wise thing to do.

Hawker followed the safest route back to the main road. He was surprised that there was no traffic on the road. Several miles behind him he could see the helicopter flying low over the back section of Williams's ranch. Its searchlight threw a brilliant white cone against the earth.

From that distance the chopper looked like some kind of weird spaceship.

Hawker slowed his pace as he reached the tree grove where he had hidden his truck. He searched the area carefully through the Star-Tron. When he was sure it was safe, he stepped into the clearing and reached for the door handle.

As he did, a flashlight inside the truck was snapped on, and Hawker could see the stainless barrel of a Colt .44 pointed at his head.

A faceless voice chuckled softly and said in an amused tone, "Well, if it ain't my wayward friend, James Hawker." The light panned across Hawker's body in slow examination. "And what do you know! Hawk, you're the first man I ever met who left for a San Antone whorehouse and came back with an extra arm!"

The man holding the revolver was Quirt Evans.

FOURTEEN

Evans motioned with the light. "Slide that nasty-looking automatic rifle off your shoulder and hand it in to me. Butt first."

Hawker did it.

"Now your side arm. What is it? A Beretta? Ah, a little Walther. Don't know why, Hawk, but I expected something a little bigger."

Evans took the automatic and laid it on the seat beside him. Still holding the Colt on him he said, "Now slide that knapsack through the window and get in."

Hawker opened the door. The dome light came on. The faded denim shirt Evans wore made his eyes look bluer, brighter, his face more sun-weathered. His blond hair was thick, molded into tight waves by the cowboy hat that sat beside him on the bench seat.

"You drive," he said. "Slow and easy, like we're headed for a Sunday picnic. You're too smart to try anything dumb, Hawk—but I'll remind you every now and then just to make sure."

Hawker closed the door and started the truck. As he backed out he said, "I figured you would be down there with Williams's other hired killers. You ought to be real proud of yourself, Quirt. You fooled me. You seemed a little too high-class to be a part of a slave ring." Hawker paused and looked at Evans closely. "And a national conspiracy."

Evans's face seemed to register more curiosity than surprise. "Me? Why, I was just down on old Skate's place to take a look at a sick foal. Little colt that had cribbed himself into a case of colic. Skate figures I'm the best horseman around, and that little colt is worth a couple hundred thousand." He smiled. "When all the shooting started, I put two and two together. Figured this nasty old pickup of yours would be hidden somewhere. Wasn't too hard to find. The open hood told me you'd disabled it as a part of your cover." He smiled. "A loose distributor wire isn't too original, Hawk."

"Why didn't you just let Jeb shoot me when he had the chance?"

"Why should I let Jeb have all the fun? Besides, I wanted to see how you dealt with Skate Williams."

"Skate might be interested to hear how loyal you are to him."

"If you ever get the chance to tell him, he might be."

"So how did you know about me, Quirt? You knew from the beginning."

"I suspected from the beginning. The way you fought Jeb threw me for a little while. Two-armed men don't fight that well with one arm. Not usually. Not unless they're James Hawker, I guess. But then I got a look at your left hand. It wasn't calloused enough. And no man wears a serape day-in, day-out in this kind of heat. And I noticed how careful you were not to undress in front of the other boys. It all added up."

"How did you know?"

"I knew. Maybe I'll tell you later." He chuckled. "If you live long enough."

"You knew, but you let me go ahead. Why?"

"You ask an awful lot of questions, Hawker."

"And you're awful shy on answers, Evans."

"Maybe it comes from doing most of my growing up in an orphanage. Answer too many questions in one of those places and they figure you're smart enough to be put in charge of some of the fun work. Scrubbing toilets. Or taking care of the babies."

They had come to the crossroad. The road seemed narrower, hazed by light rain. In the headlights the leaves in the wind looked white.

"So which way, Evans? I don't want to make a wrong turn and risk you having to shoot me before you're really ready."

"That's mighty thoughtful of you, James. Turn right."

To the left the road led back to the cattle ranch. To the right it paralleled the Williams's ranch, then led out of Star County.

Hawker started to question the order, then decided not to. If Evans wanted him to drive out of Star County, all the better.

He figured he had one chance and one chance only. The Randall attack/survival knife was still in the handmade scabbard strapped to his calf. If he could swerve the truck into a ditch, then draw the knife before Evans recovered, he might be able to put him away before he got a good shot off.

Strangely, Hawker realized he didn't want to do it. He liked Evans—even now, as he held the revolver on him. Somehow he still didn't seem to fit in with Skate Williams and his, loonies.

Hawker just couldn't picture him associated with the Mexican scum who ran the Bar of the Unknown Souls or Williams's mercenaries who would kill anybody or anything for a price. And he especially couldn't see him associated with Williams, a man who had obviously gone insane with the hunger for power.

But he would have to kill Evans. Or try. Because to fail meant his own death. And the death of Cristoba de Abella. And possibly the slower death of literally hundreds of thousands of Americans—if he was right.

And Hawker was damn sure he was right.

As he drove, Hawker began looking for a likely spot. The ditch had to be deep but not so deep that it flipped the truck. Hawker had no desire to be pinned under two tons of metal while waiting for Skate Williams to come along and finish the job.

Evans rode quietly. The Colt .44 was balanced on his lap. When he noticed Hawker looking at it, he said, "Don't be getting any wild ideas, Hawk." He reached into his pocket and drew out a tin of snuff. Copenhagen. "Want some?"

"I thought the condemned man was supposed to get anything he wanted."

"I'd offer you a cigarette, but I don't smoke."

"Me, neither."

Evans shrugged comically. "Then this is the only choice you got."

"I'll take it."

Hawker had used snuff when he'd played baseball in the Detroit farm system. That had been long ago, and he had forgotten how much he liked it.

Hawker spit out the window. The wind was cool. The rain was more of a mist, and it was warm on his face. Evans said,

"A second ago you were thinking about going for my gun, weren't you?"

"A mind reader, too, huh? You've got all sorts of talents, Evans."

He laughed. "I'm glad you didn't. Things may not be as they seem, Hawk. Don't do anything rash. Not yet."

"Just go quietly to my execution, huh? I was never very good in the lamb-to-slaughter department."

"No," Evans said wryly, "I can see that. And maybe that's why I ought to tell you now—"

Evans didn't get a chance to finish. Fifty yards ahead of them a searing white spotlight flashed on. Two soldiers stepped in front of the light, signaling for Hawker to stop.

Hawker cursed himself silently for not making his move sooner. He should have tried to jump Evans immediately. Maybe slammed the truck into a tree or something.

But now it was too late.

Now he was dead.

Unless they assumed Evans had already searched him and they took him in carrying the Randall. If they did he would talk them into a meeting with Williams. And Williams would go with him to the grave, the knife through his throat.

"Just pull over nice and easy, James," Quirt Evans said calmly. "Oh—and let me do the talking."

Hawker looked at him oddly. Evans winked. "And don't be afraid to use that nasty-looking automatic if things start getting rough."

"What in the hell—"

Evans got out and left the door open. Hawker watched as

he approached the guards. There were two who stood in front of the light, one who held the light, and several more moving around the truck behind the light.

Evans had put on his hat and had holstered his pistol. He had a long, fluid walk. His big hands were buried in his pockets. He grinned at the guards and nodded. Hawker could hear them talking through the open window.

"Evening, boys. Catch them bastards, yet?"

"Oh, it's you, Quirt. Naw. But we will. I guess they tore up the ranch pretty good. Killed a bunch of our people. Mr. Williams is steaming."

"I can't figure out why in hell they'd bother Skate. What's he got on that ranch, anyway? A bunch of money squirreled away or something?"

Hawker was surprised at the way Evans played innocent.

"Don't worry about what Mr. Williams has on his ranch," the guard said severely. "If he wants you to know, Quirt, he'll tell you."

"Okay, okay. No need to get huffy about it." Evans kicked at a rock in the road. "I'll just go on about my way. One of the boys and me are going into San Antone to get some medicine for that colt I was working on. Be back in less than two hours, I guess."

"Mr. Williams is sending you?"

"No, but he wants me to save that colt."

"We got our orders, Quirt. We're supposed to search every vehicle that comes down this road. Without exception."

Evans shrugged. "Fine with me. Search all you want. I just hope that colt hangs on. He's in a bad way, and I'd hate to have to tell Skate I missed saving him by ten minutes because you guys were just doing your job."

The guard hesitated. "The horse is in a bad way, huh?"

"He's not good. And you know how Skate feels about that foal. He's got a hundred grand wrapped up in the stud fee alone."

"Why don't you get the pilot to fly you over in the chopper if it's that important?"

"I would, but he's out playing fighter pilot. Looking for them terrorists or whatever they are. And I'll tell you, he won't be the only one to lose his job if that colt hits the high trail."

"Okay, Quirt, okay," the guard said quickly. "You can pass. But if anybody asks we searched you good."

Evans laughed as he turned and walked back toward the truck. "I'll tell 'em you didn't miss nothing but a tooth cavity and two cockroaches."

He got in the truck and closed the door. He exhaled a long breath and whispered, "Let's get the hell out of here. But not too fast."

Hawker started the truck and put it in gear.

The spotlight followed them along.

As they passed the guards the spotlight focused on Hawker's face. Hawker heard an exclamation in the background, and then the guard who had questioned Evans trotted out in front of the truck and stopped them again. He came around to the window. Hawker could see that he had his gun drawn.

"Who's your friend here, Quirt?"

The spotlight was shining into the truck. Hawker had hidden the Colt Commando under his legs. But the Walther, he noticed, was still on the seat with his knapsack.

"One of the new boys from the ranch," Evans said easily. "Name's Hawker. He's a good man with horses, so I carried him along."

The guard brought his gun up to the window. Hawker could sense the sudden tension in him, and he knew that they were going to be searched. He hoped Evans realized it.

"Is that Hawker's automatic on the seat?" Nonchalantly the guard shifted his revolver so that the barrel was pointed toward Hawker's head.

Behind him, the other guards were closing in, aware that there might be trouble. Three of them positioned themselves in front of the truck.

Evans smiled as he reached over and picked up the Walther. "This little thing?" He shifted it so that he held it by the grip smothering it in his big hand. "I guess this is yours, isn't it, James—"

Still in mid-sentence, Evans snapped off three rapid shots at point-blank range. The guard was flung backward. He clawed at his face. His husky scream was oddly muted. His mouth had been shot away.

In the same instant, Hawker and Evans cracked heads as they both ducked down in the seat. The truck's windshield exploded in on them as the guards opened up on them in unison. Somehow the door on Evans's side jolted open, and he spilled out onto the dirt road. Without hesitating, Hawker swept up the Colt Commando and dove outside, firing in mid-flight.

The three guards who stood in front of the truck were snapped backward as if yanked by a rope when the chain of slugs smacked through them. Wounded, one of them climbed feebly to his knees and raised his weapon again. Hawker squeezed off a single shot that blew his chest open.

His hands deadly calm, Hawker snapped out the spent clip. Quirt Evans lay beneath him on the dirt road.

"Quirt, are you hit?"

The tall cowboy rolled out from under Hawker's legs. His hat had been knocked off, and he rubbed his temple groggily. "Man, I've ridden Brahmans that didn't have heads as hard as yours."

Beyond the truck Hawker could hear men running. He reached up into the truck, jammed a fresh clip into the assault rifle, and stood. Two more of the soldiers were charging at them, and Hawker cut them down with two short bursts. Immediately a volley of fire that originated from behind the guards' truck sent Hawker diving for cover.

"Damn it, Quirt, you didn't answer me. Are you hit?"

Evans was sitting now, still rubbing his head. "No. But I feel like I've been axed."

Hawker knew they didn't have time to play a cat-and-mouse game with the remaining guards. He reached up into the seat, ducked another volley of fire, and pulled his knapsack down on top of him.

There were two hand grenades left, and Hawker took them both. He pulled both pins at the same time, counted a silent thousand-one, thousand-two, then, in quick succession, lobbed them overhanded toward the guards.

One landed in the bed of their stake truck, the other just beyond.

There was a deafening double explosion and a blinding white light as the phosphorous burned. Men screamed; glass burst; there was a third explosion as the heat found the gas tank of the other truck.

And then all was silent as the debris of metal and flesh rained down through the mist, leaving only the cricket *chirrr* and the rain plop of the Texas night.

Quirt Evans got shakily to his feet and drew his revolver. "We're going to have to fight our way out now, Hawk," he said groggily. "Those fuckers got artillery over there. And that last shell landed too damn close."

Hawker stood up, his assault rifle surveying the area. The stake truck no longer existed. There was only a charred frame and the smell of burned tires. Nothing recognizable as a human being remained. Hawker patted Evans's shoulder. "That was our artillery, Quirt. They're dead. All of them. We've got to get out of here."

Hawker couldn't see Evans's eyes in the darkness, but he recognized the tone in his voice. "Jesus, Hawker. All of them? Already? Man, I didn't half-believe those stories we heard about you. But now . . . *shit*."

"Who's 'we,' Quirt? Are you a cop? I know you're more than just a rodeo rider."

Evans found his hat and put it on. "I *am* a rodeo rider, Hawk. But I'm also a colonel."

Now it was Hawker's turn to be surprised. "As in the United States Army?"

"Better than that, Hawk. As in the Texas Rangers."

FIFTEEN

"Hola. . . . Buenas noches?"

"Sancho! It's James Hawker. Sorry to be calling so late."

There was the muted squall of a baby in the background.

"Ah! It is my business partner, the respected vice-president of Chicago Fossil Fuels Limited. You are checking on our progress in the great search for oil, no?"

Hawker smiled. He stood in a phone booth outside a Mobil station in Dilley, Texas. A haze of moths and mosquitoes beat themselves against the cold fluorescent light that illuminated the booth. Hawker and Evans had driven north out of Star County. When they were sure they weren't being followed, they stopped at the first small town.

"No, Sancho. I didn't call about the oil. I called about something else. I need a little help."

"Anything, my friend. You have only to ask. Is there—wait, my friend, the *chiquillo* is trying to bite our mean dog. I will be right back."

The phone clunked down, and the crying grew louder.

The Mobil station was closed. The circular awning above the fuel pumps was white and brightly lighted. In the stormy night it looked like a flying saucer descending.

A souped-up Corvette Stingray was parked in front of the station. A FOR SALE sign was taped inside the windshield. Tassels from a graduation cap hung from the rearview mirror.

It was one forty-seven A.M.

The streets of Dilley were empty.

Sancho Rigera returned to the phone. The crying had stopped. He said, "This mean dog, I will sell him when we are rich! The baby teethes on his paw, and the dog gets angry. He growls and the baby bites harder. Then he snaps, and the baby cries. Such a mean dog does not deserve to live with the president of a corporation, my friend!"

"I agree, Sancho. I'll help you sell him if you just listen for a minute."

"Yes, of course. Please continue."

"I need a place where I can get a few hours' sleep. I have a friend with me. We won't take up much room, but I need to be with people we can trust, and I also need a place to hide my truck."

"You are in trouble."

"Yes, Sancho. I'm in trouble. But it's not with the law. It is with the men who tried to force you and the others into selling the mineral rights to your property."

"Hah! The *cabrones*. I would do anything to help you." Sancho Rigera hesitated. "This friend of yours, amigo? My pretty daughter Juanita would be heartbroken if it was a woman."

"It's not a woman, Sancho. Anything but."

"Ah, that is good news. You will need food. I will have the *esposa* light the fire. We will heat some chicken and rice for you. And I have five bottles of Dos Equis beer hidden in the spring. I will get them—"

"Don't go to any trouble, Sancho. All we want to do is sleep."

"But you must stay up long enough for me to tell you about the drilling. Juan Probisco has secured four sections of good pipe—from what source, I do not know. Though it might be best not to mention it to any local police. We have already driven two of them by hand. The women in the village are upset because they no longer have a place to dump their cooking grease, but Juan Probisco says—"

"Sancho, you can tell me all about it in the morning. Please, don't wake anybody in your house. We don't want to cause you any trouble. And don't forget—we need a place to hide the truck. And, Sancho, we're also going to need some buses. Or big trucks. All you can get your hands on. Can you do that?"

"It will be done!"

Hawker smiled. "And, Sancho, don't be surprised if I look a little different to you."

"Your red hair? The *putas* have cut off your hair?"

"Better than that, Sancho. Better than that. Don't shoot if a one-armed man doesn't get out of my truck. . . ."

SIXTEEN

It had been a long ride on horseback, but there was no other choice. Williams's men would have heard cars. They would have been ready.

There were drawbacks to working with a team, but there were also advantages. And when it came to working with the Texas Rangers, the advantages far outweighed the drawbacks.

Quirt Evans had talked Hawker into it on the way to Sancho Rigera's. And then he had talked some more while they wolfed down hot chicken and yellow rice, served by the shy-eyed and lovely Juanita Rigera.

Evans based his argument on one often repeated truth: The Texas Rangers are no ordinary law-enforcement agency.

Hawker already knew that. He had read enough about the Rangers and, in fact, had done a term paper on the organization while working on his B.A. in Law Enforcement. He knew the history almost as well as Evans.

The Rangers was a band of rugged mounted riflemen organized in the early 1800s to protect American settlers from Indians and Mexican bandits. Unlike the U.S. Cavalry, the Rangers used the methods of their enemies to fight. One noted Texas politician summarized their abilities this way: "The Texas Ranger can ride like a Mexican, trail like an Indian, shoot like a Tennessean, and fight like the very devil."

They were, in fact, America's first guerrilla fighters.

During the Mexican War of the 1840s, the federal government established forts along the Texas frontier and garrisoned them with regular troops. But Sam Houston, speaking in the U.S. Senate, asked that they be sent home. They didn't need an army to defeat Mexico, said Houston. After all, they had one thousand Texas Rangers—and they were enough.

Hawker knew most of the Rangers' celebrated history, and he had heard that the modern-day Rangers were not much different from the Rangers of old. They still wore no uniforms. They still furnished their own transportation and weaponry. And they were still rugged individualists known for preferring quick thinking to force—but who could use deadly force, if need be, like few others in the world of law enforcement.

So when Quirt Evans said he could have ten fully equipped Rangers, complete with court warrants, at the Rigera ranch within six hours, Hawker consented.

As Evans reasoned, "If what you say about Skate Williams and his food franchise chain is true, Hawk, then we damn well can't take the chance of his getting away. We've got to get him."

"It's true, Quirt. I'm sure of it. You saw the leaves I brought back from the greenhouses at Ranch Number Three. Hell, it took me longer to recognize them than it did you. Jonathan Flischmann found out—and they murdered him. It's the only thing that makes sense. Williams could have beaten a slavery rap. You know that."

Evans's mouth was grim. "I know, Hawk, I know. I spent a year and a half infiltrating the operation and gaining that bastard's confidence, only to realize that his Hispanic slaves would never testify against him. They live in too much fear. To a court of law they would just look like more wetbacks content with any damn work they could find."

Hawker was impressed. "A year and a half? You must really have it in for that guy."

Evans gave him a strange look. "You don't know the half of it, Hawk. Skate Williams is a psychopath. Cares about no one but himself. If it took ten years I'd still get the bastard."

Hawker nodded and said nothing. There was something in the big Ranger's tone that said he didn't care to talk about it anymore.

So Hawker drifted off to a fitful sleep while Quirt Evans went to work on the phone. Before calling his fellow Rangers, he contacted the state patrol and notified them of the shipment that might have left Williams's ranch despite Hawker's attack. Then he went to work waking up state officials. They were prim and officious until Evans told them what it was about—and then they were outraged with disbelief.

Finally he placed a call to the governor. The governor was asleep, of course. Evans insisted that he be awakened.

Ten minutes later the governor returned his call. At first the governor refused to believe him. And then the disbelief became shock. And the shock became disappointment.

The Governor admitted that he loved Rio Bravo Burgers. He

said now he understood why he felt "antsy" if he didn't have them at least a couple of times a week. . . .

James Hawker awoke late in the morning. Outside Sancho Rigera's adobe ranch house, he pumped water over his head.

The sun was pale yellow, flat against the old western sky.

Juanita Rigera and her mother were washing clothes in a wooden tub. He noticed the graceful lines of the girl. Her blue-black hair was tied in a ponytail, and she wore a white cotton dress that emphasized the tautness of her body. She was lovely indeed, and seeing her made him think of Cristoba.

Tonight, he thought. *You'll be free tonight.*

Hawker found Sancho in a sand-and-cactus swale just beyond the village. He and a dozen other men squatted on their haunches, Mexican-fashion, before a makeshift oil drilling rig.

The men wore no shirts, and they glistened with sweat.

They had planted four old telephone poles as the rig's foundation. High atop the poles was a platform and a block and tackle. Hooked to the block and tackle was a chunk of metal that must have weighed two hundred pounds. Centered beneath it was a section of long pipe fitted with a high-tensile-strength driving head so that the pipe would not split.

Hawker wondered where Juan Probisco had stolen it.

Before they would allow Hawker to organize them into a truck caravan for the night's assault, they insisted on giving their "honored vice-president" of Chicago Fossil Fuels Ltd. a tour of the operation.

Hawker humored them. They joked about his growing a new

arm. They suggested that the black eye and swollen face were not the result of a fistfight but of a passionate love affair instead. Hawker laughed, enjoying their company. He complimented their efforts at great length. And why not?

After all, in a few hours they would be risking their lives to free people they had never met.

Shortly afterward, the ten Texas Rangers arrived. Probably because he had seen too many late-night westerns, Hawker expected them to come by horse, dusty after a hard ride.

Instead they arrived in immaculately kept trucks, their horses in trailers behind.

The Rangers varied in shape and size, but they all seemed to have that ruddy, rugged look of humor and confidence that he had first liked in the face of Quirt Evans.

It was Evans who called them together for a briefing. It was Evans who showed them maps of the Williams's ranch, told them how they would present the search warrant to the guards, and what the next steps would be if the guards refused to let them pass.

Hawker was only briefly introduced, and then only as a private citizen who would be going along because of his familiarity with the area.

But Hawker could see that the other Rangers knew who he was. Could see it in their eyes. And he understood why Evans had gone out of his way to purposely ignore him. It was for his own protection. So that later, when the Senate committee of investigation was formed, he would be just a faceless, nameless man none of them remembered.

Or pretended not to remember.

They left at dusk, the horses saddled and fed in the trailers behind the trucks that they would drive to the Star County line.

Just before they pulled out, Hawker placed a long-distance call to Andrea Marie Flischmann.

He wanted to tell her he had found her brother's murderer.

There was no answer.

SEVENTEEN

So it had been a long ride. Especially for Hawker, who was no horseman.

Twice on the narrow dirt road to Williams's estate fast trucks had passed them but paid them no mind.

The horses were disguises in and of themselves.

To people in the trucks the twelve men on horseback probably just looked like wranglers from Ranch #4.

Fortunately they couldn't see what the riders were carrying in their saddlebags and beneath the rolled tarps.

Hawker wore a black cotton watch sweater, jeans, and worn Nike running shoes. His face and hands still hurt from the fights he had had the night before. Evans had found him a gray, weathered cowboy hat with a rattlesnake band. The knapsack stuffed with ordnance was strapped to the back of the broad-chested Arabian he rode.

When the guardhouse and high adobe fence came into view, they pulled into tighter formation, two abreast. Three hundred yards from the guardhouse, the bright searchlight flashed on. Hawker shielded his eyes and looked at Evans.

"You still insist on trying to serve that damn warrant?"

Evans winked, but Hawker sensed fear behind the calm facade. "That's the law, Hawk. That's what I get paid for."

"You don't get paid to die, Quirt. And that's just what's going to happen. Once they know you're a Ranger, you won't make it three steps from the guardhouse. Why in the hell go through the formalities?"

Evans smiled as he kicked his horse ahead. "I think you know. You were a cop once. And a damn good one, from what I've heard. You would have done the same thing, Hawk."

As Hawker watched his friend trot toward his rendezvous with the guards—and probably death—he pulled open his knapsack. From it he took an electronic detonating device. It was about the size of a television remote control. But instead of buttons on its face there was a frequency dial and two toggle switches. Hawker set the frequency, then took a flare gun from the knapsack. He snapped it open and inserted a single 12-gauge-size signal cartridge.

The searchlight followed Evans as he pulled up to the guardhouse: a single man on horseback. Ol' Quirt. The trail boss who worked over at Ranch #4 and sometimes came to doctor Skate Williams's horses. There would be perfunctory smiles and thoughts of conversation.

But then they would notice that Quirt had changed. They would see there was something different about him.

It was the badge on his chest: the shield that identified him as a Texas Ranger.

And then they would have to kill him.

Hawker watched nervously as Evans slid down off his horse. Behind him, Hawker heard the rifle bolt click as the other Rangers readied their weapons to provide covering fire.

The two guards stepped out to meet Evans. Hawker was aware of movement behind the guardhouse: four or five more soldiers waiting in the darkness. He saw Quirt Evans reach into his shirt and pull out the warrant. Holding it in both hands, one of the guards turned into the light so he could read it.

And then everything happened very damn quickly indeed.

There was a blur of movement, and the guard holding the paper went for his holstered automatic. But Evans got to his Colt faster, and there were two sledgehammer *kerwhacks*, and the guard was blown backward into the adobe wall.

As the second guard went for his gun Hawker fired the flare. It exploded over Skate Williams's mansion with a fiery red light. It was beneath that weird crimson glow that Hawker saw Evans drop the other guard with a single shot, then turn to run to his horse. As he ran, the soldiers materialized from the shadows. They opened fire on Evans.

Quirt stumbled, spun, and fell. Somehow he managed to get up on his horse. Sitting at a sickening angle, he kicked his horse into a gallop away from the guardhouse.

Hawker didn't hesitate. He hit the first toggle switch, and the guardhouse was pulverized by a blinding yellow explosion. The impact threw the soldiers high into the air. Backlighted by the fiery glow, they looked like tumbling rag dolls.

Hawker's Arabian spooked as the other Rangers charged by him; the Rangers leaned low over their horses, reins in their teeth, automatic rifles in their hands. They galloped through the hole where the guardhouse had been, and when more soldiers materialized from the shadows, they opened fire.

Hawker changed the frequency on the detonator and touched the second toggle switch.

The explosion was more like an earthquake. It came in a rib-cage-vibrating series: first the processing plant; then Williams's mansion, the back wall, and the fence outside the slave quarters went up. Then the tank of red gas apparently detonated another tank, and still another. Somewhere within the plant was a store of munitions, and these, too, went off, sputtering and whacking and flaring.

Hawker no longer needed moonlight by which to see. An orange, gaseous ball of fire roared high above the trees, illuminating the whole estate.

From within the compound Hawker could hear the high shrieks of agony mixing with the battle whoops of the Rangers as they cut through the panicking mercenaries.

He hoped none of the shrieks came from Quirt Evans. He had been hit, there was no doubt about that. How bad, there was no way of finding out until it was over.

And that wouldn't take long.

Hawker's assault the night before had softened them. And now it became quickly obvious that the mercenaries didn't have the heart to stand toe-to-toe with a fast-moving band of hell fighters on horseback.

In the heat-charged light, Hawker could see that the soldiers were both running and fighting—but mostly running.

He just hoped the escaping slaves didn't run into the

fleeing soldiers. If they didn't, if they kept their heads, they should have been able to find their way through the ruptured back wall and to the first dirt road—where Sancho Rigera and the other men from the village would be waiting with their trucks.

Hawker put the detonator and flare gun into the knapsack and pulled the Colt Commando from the rifle scabbard attached to the saddle. Then he kicked the Arabian into a smooth canter and rode into the estate grounds. Unlike the Rangers, he wasn't a good enough horseman to fight from a saddle, so he dropped to the ground and let the horse go free.

Before him, the ground floor of Skate Williams's mansion was aflame. Hawker was tempted to fight his way upstairs to make sure Williams wasn't hiding there.

But there was something else he had to do first. Something he had waited too long to do. . . .

With the Colt held at hip level Hawker sprinted around the burning house and through the ornamental garden where he had killed the guard the night before.

The cottage that imprisoned Cristoba de Abella was brightly lighted. It looked snug and neat and safe in the shadows of the trees.

Hawker knew better.

There was the silhouette of a man against the front curtains. A gigantic man. He made a familiar motion with his hands, which Hawker recognized immediately: Skate Williams was buckling his belt.

Not unbuckling it. Buckling it.

Hawker lengthened his stride, running hard toward the front porch. Too hard.

He didn't expect any guards to be still standing at their posts. He was wrong.

As he came charging down the path, a single figure stepped out in front of him. The figure was holding something in his hand. A gun. A military .45 automatic.

Hawker was going too fast to stop. He collided with the figure, and a microsecond later, the automatic spewed fire. Hawker felt a sledgehammerlike blow against his left thigh. And then he was tumbling, falling, his whole left leg numb. He knew he had been shot, but he didn't have time to worry about how bad it was.

The figure was on top of him, pummeling him with his fists, and then the barrel of the .45 was pointed directly at his face. Hawker knocked it aside with his left elbow just as it exploded a second time, and he hit the man in the face with a sizzling right hand.

The man tumbled over backward, still holding on to the .45. Hawker smothered him with his body, then cracked him with two more rights. Through his broken mouth the guard half-cried, "I'll blow your fucking head off for that, you bastard!"

The voice hit one of his memory electrodes, and Hawker realized it was Roy Dalton, the manager of Ranch #4, the sour-looking man with the black mustache who had hired him.

Why would he be outside the cottage guarding it for Williams?

And then the answer came. He wasn't standing guard while Williams raped Cristoba—he had probably been involved in it.

A treat awarded him by his employer, like throwing a dog a biscuit.

Dalton brought the automatic up once again, but Hawker locked his hands around the man's wrist and turned it until he heard the delicate carpus bones pop. As Dalton's wrist gave way the .45 swung downward and went off.

Beneath him, Dalton kicked wildly, then lay still.

Half of his face had been shot away.

Hawker rolled off the corpse and touched his thigh. The wound was not bad. Blood seeped out steadily, but the artery had not been shot away. The slug apparently had cut a swath of flesh away on a downward course, narrowly missing his right foot.

The pain was beginning to come now: a deep, throbbing ache.

He pulled out the metal stock on the Colt Commando and, using the weapon as a short crutch, got shakily to his feet. He fully expected to see Skate Williams standing on the porch, a gun in his hand.

But the porch was empty, the front door open.

Hawker knew that if the front door was not locked, Cristoba would be gone.

He hobbled up the front steps, anyway, and looked inside.

For long nights afterward he would wish that he had not.

The girl lay inside on the bed. She lay on her back. The sheer white nightgown had been ripped from her body. Her breasts were paler than her shoulders, and they were flattened and rounded by their own weight.

Williams had been here, all right. And Dalton, too. Maybe

others. Hawker wondered how long the horror had gone on for her.

Her nut-colored legs, long and graceful, were smeared with dried blood that had pooled in splotches beneath her on the sheet. There were scratch marks on her neck and arms. A great many scratch marks.

Yes, it had gone on a long time. Gone on and on until Cristoba had finally ended it by her own hand.

The pillow beneath her head was soggy with blood. Unlike the blood on her legs, it was fresh. Her right fist was locked around the butt of a .38-caliber Smith & Wesson revolver. The pressure of the slug entering her right ear had blown her facial structure into a bloated mask of horror. Only her eyes remained oddly unchanged: dull brown orbs that bespoke great knowledge but no emotion; bespoke the inexorable understanding of her ancient people, as if all the tragedy, madness, and cruelty of life was beneath their comment.

Hawker heard a weak, involuntary sob and realized that it originated within him.

Why hadn't she used the gun on Williams? Or one of the others?

He would never know.

He hobbled across the room and touched her eyelids, closing them, then covered her with a sheet.

"I'm sorry, Cristoba," he whispered. "You should have never trusted me. I'm so damn sorry."

Hawker stood over the ruined body of the girl for another anguished moment before turning and leaving at a fast hobble, punishing himself with the agony of using his left leg.

Outside, the stars were a brilliant veil above the orange haze of smoke from the fires that now consumed the ranch. In the air was the stink of burning gasoline, and the flames glowed eerily above the trees.

Hawker thought he had been to hell before.

But nothing had ever quite compared to this.

Hawker headed off into the shadows along the path that led to the factory. He half-ran, dragging his left leg along behind.

Skate Williams couldn't have gotten far. And when he found him, Hawker would show him what hell was all about. He would show him and show him and show him. . . .

EIGHTEEN

Skate Williams jumped him as he passed the first greenhouse, coming out of the shadows like a grizzly, all arms and fists and beefy weight, knocking Hawker to the ground.

Hawker had been slowly wilting from shock and loss of blood. He knew he could not go much farther. He had, in fact, begun to rationalize the urge to lay down and rest. He told himself his mission had been a success in one way—the slave compound had been empty when he'd passed it. They had all escaped. And what would happen if he *did* find Williams? He was too weak to do anything but simply shoot him, and Hawker wanted to make it last a hell of a lot longer than that.

But then he remembered the girl. Remembered the way she looked when she was alive. Remembered the tilt of her head, the glint of her brown eyes, and the fine bravery in her that night outside the Bar of the Unknown Souls.

Then Hawker remembered the way Williams had left her. And suddenly, the weariness and weakness were gone, fired by his own fresh anger.

A moment later Williams took him by complete surprise. He hit Hawker four strides into a lumbering sprint, hit him waist-high with his massive right shoulder. The impact catapulted the Colt Commando from his hands, snapped his head sideways, and almost knocked him out.

It took Hawker a dizzy moment to realize who his attacker was. By the time he did, Williams was diving for the assault rifle, his own revolver obviously out of ammunition.

He half-landed on Hawker, his hands outstretched toward the Commando. His body stank of sweat and cigar smoke, and the weight of him all but knocked the wind out of the vigilante. Hawker rolled painfully to his side and caught Williams's right arm, pulling it away. Williams clubbed at him with his left fist, but Hawker managed to swing his head away from the blows. If one landed, Hawker knew, he would be knocked out. The man must have weighed close to three hundred and fifty pounds.

Using all his strength, Hawker forced the huge Texan's right arm under him, then slid from beneath the man, pulling his right arm up between his shoulder blades.

When Williams tried to struggle out of the hammerlock, Hawker put more pressure on the arm.

"I want you to remember something before I kill you," Hawker hissed, his breath coming in labored gasps. "I want you to remember Cristoba de Abella. I want you to remember the way she looked when you left her, because you're going to look twice as bad when you die, Williams. You're going to be such a mess, the crows won't even bother with you."

Beneath him, Skate Williams winced with pain. The left side of his face dug a furrow in the sand as he edged himself along, trying to relieve the pressure on his arm. "Look, you don't got to kill me. I got money. I got a lot of money." There was a piggish whimper in his voice that nauseated Hawker. "You say you're going to kill me because of that girl? Well, shit, boy, a couple hundred thousand in cash can do a lot to wipe out a memory."

"Forget it, Williams," Hawker said. He felt the urge to kill him then and there, but he didn't want it to end that quickly. Instead he increased the pressure on the big man's arm until Williams began to make a strange noise. It was the mosquito-whine a balloon makes when you stretch the valve between your fingers. It took Hawker a moment to realize that the man was crying. Hawker said, "I know all about how you made that money, and I know all about your fast-food franchise, and why they're getting so popular so quick." Williams struggled beneath him, and Hawker settled him with even more pressure. "I've visited this experimental farm, friend. I know what you grow here, and I know what you do with it. Money from oil and cattle wasn't enough. You wanted to control it all, Williams. Instead of just slave workers, you wanted to control a nation of slaves."

Goaded by the pain, Williams gave an unexpected thrust of his pelvis that threw Hawker off-balance. Then he kicked backward and caught Hawker flush on his injured thigh with the heel of his boot. In sudden agony Hawker released his grip for just a moment.

That's all it took.

Williams cracked Hawker hard with his elbow, then came up standing, the Colt Commando leveled at Hawker's stomach. "Now it's your turn to beg, you son of a bitch," Williams bellowed. "And you'd better beg long and hard, because I'm going to blow your fucking guts right out." A strange chuckle escaped his lips. It was the frenzied laughter of a psychopath who realizes, much to his delight, that once again he has outwitted his enemies.

"You say I wanted control? Well, you're wrong there, buddy boy, 'cause I already *got* control. I got the money, I got the army, and in another two years' time people are going to be fightin' in line just to get to them little food stands of mine." He laughed again. "You know where I got the idea? It's damn near funny! Hell, I got it from Coca Cola! Back at the turn of the century they used cocaine in Coca Cola. Had to ship the coca leaves up from South America, but they used it just the same. Damn profitable business until people started catching on that they didn't just *like* Coca Cola, they *had* to have it. Hell, they were addicted. 'Course, the damn government came along and made them change the ingredients.

"No one else took up the idea until I came along. Five years ago, some old boy approached me about financing a fast-food franchise. Said putting barbecue sauce on hamburgers would be the biggest thing since McDonald's." The huge, piggish face contorted into a grin. "Well, I made damn sure it was *bigger* than McDonald's. Started my own coca tree farm. Needed people who'd refine the shit and not talk—so I started bringing in wetback slaves. We toyed around with the idea of putting it in the sauce. But there was too much waste in that, so we just put it right in with the ground meat. Knew I could buy off the inspectors. And you know what? The dumb fucking public went for it! Hell, I got more stands in Houston than McDonald's does!

149

Getting inquiries from all over the country about the franchise. 'Course, the problem there is finding inspectors in every state who can be bought off. But we will, by God! And when that day comes, sluts like Cristoba what's-her-name will climb up my steps on their bellies just to get another little fix.'"

Hawker had gotten slowly to his feet. If he was going to die, he was going to die standing. He said, "You're pathetic, Williams. Go ahead and kill me—but don't do it thinking you're going to be in the clear. I've told too many people about your operation. And how you killed Jonathan Flischmann to keep him from talking. He knew, too, didn't he, Williams?"

The fat man made a pained expression. "That little Jew twerp? He didn't have enough sense to know when to call it quits. Hell, I offered him money. Plenty of money. When he refused, I sent Roy Dalton up to find him." Williams smiled. "Roy found him, all right. Gave him the Smith & Wesson cure for insomnia." He raised the assault rifle, and his expression changed. "Just like I'm going to give you—"

"No, you're not," said a voice from the shadows. From behind one of the greenhouses stepped Quirt Evans. He held his left arm and shoulder at an odd angle, and Hawker knew how badly wounded he must be. But his voice was strong, and his stainless Colt .44 was aimed at Williams's back. Evans said calmly, "You shoot, Skate, and it'll be the last thing you ever do."

Williams raised one eyebrow. He kept the assault rifle on Hawker and did not turn around. "Quirt? That you? Shit, boy, you can't shoot me. I'm your damn—"

"I know who you are," Evans cut in. "And you can bet I'll shoot you."

"And what if I told you to drop it or I'll blow this character into the next county?"

"That's your decision to make, Skate. He doesn't mean nothing to me. Says he's from Chicago, and I've never met anyone worth a shit from the Midwest. You go right on and shoot if you want to, Skate. But from the distance I'm standing, I reckon this .44 of mine, hitting you the way I got her aimed, would probably take your head right off. Now, I've heard a couple of theories about what happens when a head comes off real quick like. I've heard the person dies instantly, with no thoughts about nothing. But I've also heard that the head just lays there for three or four minutes, thinking like hell until the oxygen runs out. 'Course, no one really knows for sure. But you're a clever guy, Skate. Maybe you could find a way to let me know while your head's on the ground. Maybe wink at me or something."

Very slowly Williams turned to face Quirt Evans. "You're not going to shoot me, Quirt. You ain't got the balls to do it."

Hawker waited expectantly for Evans to prove him wrong. But then he saw Quirt's face change; saw the color grow pale; saw the jaw drop slack; saw his blue eyes grow round with fear and surprise—surprise that he could not pull the trigger.

Williams laughed. "You're like most of these modern-day Texas cowboys, Quirt—all hat and boots. Now, you put that handgun down like a good boy—"

It took Hawker three agonizing strides to get to him. The heavy Randall attack/survival knife was cool in his hand. He threw himself on Williams's back and spun him around. Williams got the Colt up to fire, but Hawker knocked it aside and smashed his nose flat with a hard left. As Williams's head snapped back, Hawker drove the seven-and-a-half-inch blade deep through the fat and gristle of his throat.

Williams made a loud, gagging sound as he staggered around and around in small circles, clawing at the knife. Then he stopped, his pale eyes growing bleary. The pale eyes found Hawker, staring at him with bleak reappraisal, before he collapsed on the ground.

Mechanically Hawker extracted his knife and cleaned the blade in the soft Texas earth. He turned to the tall Texas Ranger. "He was going to kill you. Why didn't you shoot?"

Quirt Evans sagged wearily against the bracing of the greenhouse. "I had a father once," he said, his voice suddenly weak and distant. "A young millionaire from Dallas who ran out on my mother." He looked at the huge corpse on the ground. "He's dead now, Hawk. And I'm glad."

NINETEEN

Three weeks after Hawker got out of Houston General Hospital, and one week after Quirt Evans was released from the same hospital, the two men sat on wooden stools in the sun by the stone well outside Sancho Rigera's house.

It was one of those summer days in Texas that seemed more like a winter day in southern Mexico: The air so dry that it turned the sky to blue powder and the hills and buttes to stratified layers of rust and copper and bronze.

The house was made of white adobe, and it reflected the heat of the sun onto their backs. To Quirt Evans, who had been shot twice in the back, it felt especially good.

Hawker took the last swallow of beer from the dark bottle of Dos Equis and held it up to the sun. Watching him, Quirt Evans smiled. "Is that a toast or a signal?"

Behind them the screen door slammed closed, and the lovely Juanita Rigera patted Hawker tenderly on the head before exchanging the empty bottle for a fresh one, cold from the new refrigerator inside.

"A signal," said Hawker, sipping the beer with real pleasure.

Evans looked offended. He tugged at the girl's white skirt. *"Señorita,"* he said. *"Yo quiero una cerveza fria, por favor."*

Juanita flipped her ponytail at him impishly, planted her hands on her hips, and wagged off.

"Does that means she's going to bring me a beer?" Evans asked with comic concern. "I mean, I deserve one. After all I've been through, and saving your life not just once . . ."

"Uh, oh," moaned Hawker.

". . . but twice, and putting my neck on the line just so some has-been from Chicago . . ."

"Do I have to hear this again?"

". . . can come back to the *hacienda* and sit around on his butt and play the hero."

Hawker held out the bottle of Dos Equis. "Here. Take mine. I'll get another."

Evans became suddenly aloof. "Hah! I'm not going to drink after you." His face described distaste. "You've got snuff in your mouth."

"Well, so do you, for God's sake."

The two men looked at each other, then broke out laughing; laughing until the tears came. Evans leaned over painfully, still not quite recovered from his wounds. "Hey, that little girl really likes you, Hawk. I know it's none of my business, but you've been here two weeks, and I was just wondering if you and she are . . . an item?"

"You're right," said Hawker. "It *is* none of your business. And, no we aren't. Not really."

"Yeah? And what's that supposed to mean."

Hawker laughed. "Last night I went out for a walk. She was waiting for me. Waiting in the moonlight. We talked—me with my bad Spanish. We laughed. And, Quirt, I hadn't really laughed since long before I ran into the late Skate Williams. We held hands. She gave me a peck on the cheek. And that was it."

Evans raised his eyebrows. "To these people that means you're practically engaged."

Hawker checked his watch and said nothing. It was eleven-twenty. Sancho Rigera was more than an hour late. Considering the circumstances, though, it was understandable. And forgivable.

Evans had arrived that morning, a very pleasant surprise.

Hawker changed the subject. "So the court hearings went okay, Quirt? Gas Blakely didn't make any waves?"

Evans had forgotten he had Hawker's beer, and he took a swig. "Smooth as silk, Hawk. You hardly figured into the testimony. Here's the way it went. The Texas Rangers went to a private residence with a search warrant. We came under heavy fire and returned the fire. A number of people were killed during the conflict—fortunately none of our men. One hundred and eighty-three people held as slaves were freed, and they were taken away by the brave citizens of this village. The governor closed down the Rio Bravo franchises almost immediately. The state lab boys tested the beef and projected that only a very small number of consumers might have trouble kicking the cocaine monkey. State Services has opened its doors, offering free treatment to anyone who thinks they need it. Actually it was a blessing in disguise. A fair number of closet junkies have jumped on the opportunity to get help because they can go for treatment and tell their neighbors that getting hooked really wasn't their fault at all."

Hawker smiled. So his mission was a success. Again. Once more the luck had held, the bullets had missed their marks, and he had lived to hold a chilled beer in the fresh heat of a new day.

But the luck could not last.

In the back of his mind James Hawker knew that. One day the mission would come that was too tough. Or find him when the luck was not with him. And he, too, would travel the blinding white passage into death that so many of his enemies had.

Hawker checked his watch again, then got slowly to his feet. "I've got a phone call to make," he said.

"Hawk," Evans said quickly. Hawker stopped and looked at his friend. Evans looked oddly uneasy. "Hawk, there's another reason I came down here. Two other reasons, actually."

"Yeah? You name it, Quirt."

"Well . . . the first thing is about Skate. Skate Williams, you know."

"I know who you mean," Hawker put in wryly.

"Look, no one else knows that he was my . . . that we were related, and I—"

"I haven't told a soul, Quirt. And I don't intend to."

Evans looked immediately relieved. "I appreciate that, Hawk. I really do. Whenever I think of that fat bastard, I get chills."

"The second thing, Quirt? What is it?"

Evans was no longer uneasy. "Well, I was talking to the other boys, Hawk. The Rangers, I mean. We're a pretty small group. And we like it that way. We're damn selective about who we let in and, well, we were just wondering if you might be interested in joining up." Before Hawker could react, Evans held up one finger. "But first you have to understand that we do everything by the book, Hawk. I know' I don't have to explain that to you. But if you're interested we'd be damn proud to have you."

Hawker leaned against the chair, genuinely touched. "Quirt, I appreciate it. You know I mean that." He hesitated, searching for the right words. "But we all have our jobs to do in this world, and I'm afraid my job is pretty well charted out for me. But if I were going to join any force, you can be damn sure it would be the Rangers." He squeezed his friend's arm. "Thanks, Quirt." He studied the nearly empty bottle in Evans's hand. "I'll bring you another beer—when you get done with mine."

Evans was laughing as Hawker went into the house and picked up the phone.

Andrea Marie Flischmann, his ex-wife, answered on the third ring. Hawker had talked to her twice since the assault on Williams's ranch. In their last conversation he had asked Andrea to come to Texas and take a vacation with him. Maybe rent a car and drive down to Mexico. Spend some long days on the beaches—and some longer nights in bed. As an added incentive Hawker had mentioned that she might find some interesting artwork for her shop. She had insisted they both give it some thought before deciding. After all, they had already been married once, and it hadn't worked.

Hawker could tell immediately from the tone of her voice that the answer was no.

"James? Is that you?" She sounded formal, uncomfortable. "You sound like you're a million miles away."

From the phone Hawker could see Juanita Rigera standing over the counter in the kitchen. He studied the pretty way the sun caught her face as she rolled out the cornmeal for the evening's tortillas. There was something in her cheek structure that reminded him of someone else; another Indio beauty who had been swept away from her home by the horror of a single madman. "A million miles away?" he said, smiling to himself. "I guess I am. Almost."

"James," she began, "I feel so badly about what I'm going to say. Especially after all you did for me . . . my family . . . taking care of Jonathan's killer. It was such a relief to hear."

"I know, Andrea. And you're not coming down, are you?"

Her voice was small. "No, James. I'm not. There's a big show in Paris this week, and I'm flying over with . . . a friend."

"A friend?"

"A friend. Bill Herald. A very fine young artist. It will do us both good, and he'll learn a lot."

Hawker repressed the urge to say, "I'll bet." Instead he said, "That's fine, Andrea. I'm glad for you, and it restores my faith in the art world. At least some artists appreciate a beautiful woman."

Now her laughter was genuine. "He does, Hawk. The boy truly does."

For the next few minutes they made small talk. Hawker filled her in on some surprising new details, and just before he hung up he heard cars coming down the road.

He looked out the window. A line of six new Cadillacs in six different and startling colors threw a whirlwind of dust in their wake as they floated down the rutted lane and skidded into the sand yard.

Juanita came up from behind him, a wide-eyed look of awe on her face. Hawker noticed how naturally she fitted herself under his thick arm and blushed when he kissed her on the cheek.

"The cars!" she gasped in thick English. "Are they not beautiful?"

Behind the line of Cadillacs, Chicago Fossil Fuels's new oil derrick towered. Only partially built, it still dwarfed the jury-rigged structure that Sancho and Juan and the others had used to pierce the shallow anticline; the hand-driven drill, which, after long weeks of hard work and many beers, began to spew up a black, liquid substance that had absolutely nothing to do with the cooking habits of the women in the village.

The men from the state regulatory agency had been enthusiastic. They estimated the well would pump more than twice an average well's production: about twenty-eight barrels, day-in, day-out. And they had little doubt there were other deposits beneath the poor village. They also suggested Chicago Fossil Fuels hire a production team, a good bookkeeper—and maybe consider putting in a bid on the Skate Williams estate, which would soon be put up for auction by the courts.

Sancho Rigera, looking slightly drunk but dapper in a black derby, waved wildly out the window of his new car. "James, my friend!" he yelled. "We are rich! Rich, I tell you. We went into town and bought many cases of beer, and Juan Probisco did not steal a thing!"

Beside him, Juanita clasped her hands together in delight. She looked at Hawker, an ageless fire in her eyes. "In this new automobile I would like to be going for a ride tonight." She sighed dramatically. "But I do not know how to drive."

Hawker squeezed her and smiled. "My friend out there, the tall ugly one in the cowboy hat, can drive. But you'll have to bring a date for him. And she must be pretty. Very pretty."

Juanita Rigera squealed with delight and trotted off toward the telephone. "There is this girl, a friend, Lorena Hernandez. A woman of the world who has been even to San Antone!"

Hawker went out onto the porch. Quirt Evans looked up expectantly. "Hey, where's my beer?"

Hawker patted his shoulder. "Save your energy, friend. You may need it."

Evans tilted his cowboy hat back. "What?"

Hawker found that he was laughing. Laughing very hard. "Lorena will explain it to you," he said, wiping his eyes. "But be careful. I'm not sure even a colonel in the Rangers is ready for a girl who has been to San Antone."

"San Antonio?" Evans wagged his eyebrows. "I haven't been to Flora and Ella's in a long time." He got up and stretched, smiling. "In fact, I might even take me a little nap just so I'll be ready. . . ."

ABOUT THE AUTHOR

Randy Wayne White was born in Ashland, Ohio, in 1950. Best known for his series featuring retired NSA agent Doc Ford, he has published over twenty crime fiction and nonfiction adventure books. White began writing while working as a fishing guide in Florida, where most of his books are set. His earlier writings include the Hawker series, which he published under the pen name Carl Ramm. White has received several awards for his fiction, and his novels have been featured on the *New York Times* bestseller list. He was a monthly columnist for *Outside* magazine and has contributed to several other publications, as well as lectured throughout the United States and travelled extensively. White currently lives on Pine Island in South Florida, and remains an active member of the community through his involvement with local civic affairs as well as the restaurant Doc Ford's Sanibel Rum Bar and Grill.

HAWKER EBOOKS

FROM OPEN ROAD MEDIA

OPEN ROAD
INTEGRATED MEDIA

OPEN ROAD

INTEGRATED MEDIA

Open Road Integrated Media is a digital publisher and multimedia content company. Open Road creates connections between authors and their audiences by marketing its ebooks through a new proprietary online platform, which uses premium video content and social media.

Videos, Archival Documents, and New Releases

Sign up for the Open Road Media newsletter and get news delivered straight to your inbox.

Sign up now at
www.openroadmedia.com/newsletters